# RAFE: FIREBRAND COWBOYS

BARB HAN

TORJAKE PUBLISHING

Copyright © 2023 by Barb Han

All rights reserved.

No part of this book may be reproduced in any form or by any electronic or mechanical means, including information storage and retrieval systems, without written permission from the author, except for the use of brief quotations in a book review.

Editing: Ali Williams

Cover Design: Jacob's Cover Designs

*To my family for being the great loves of my life.*

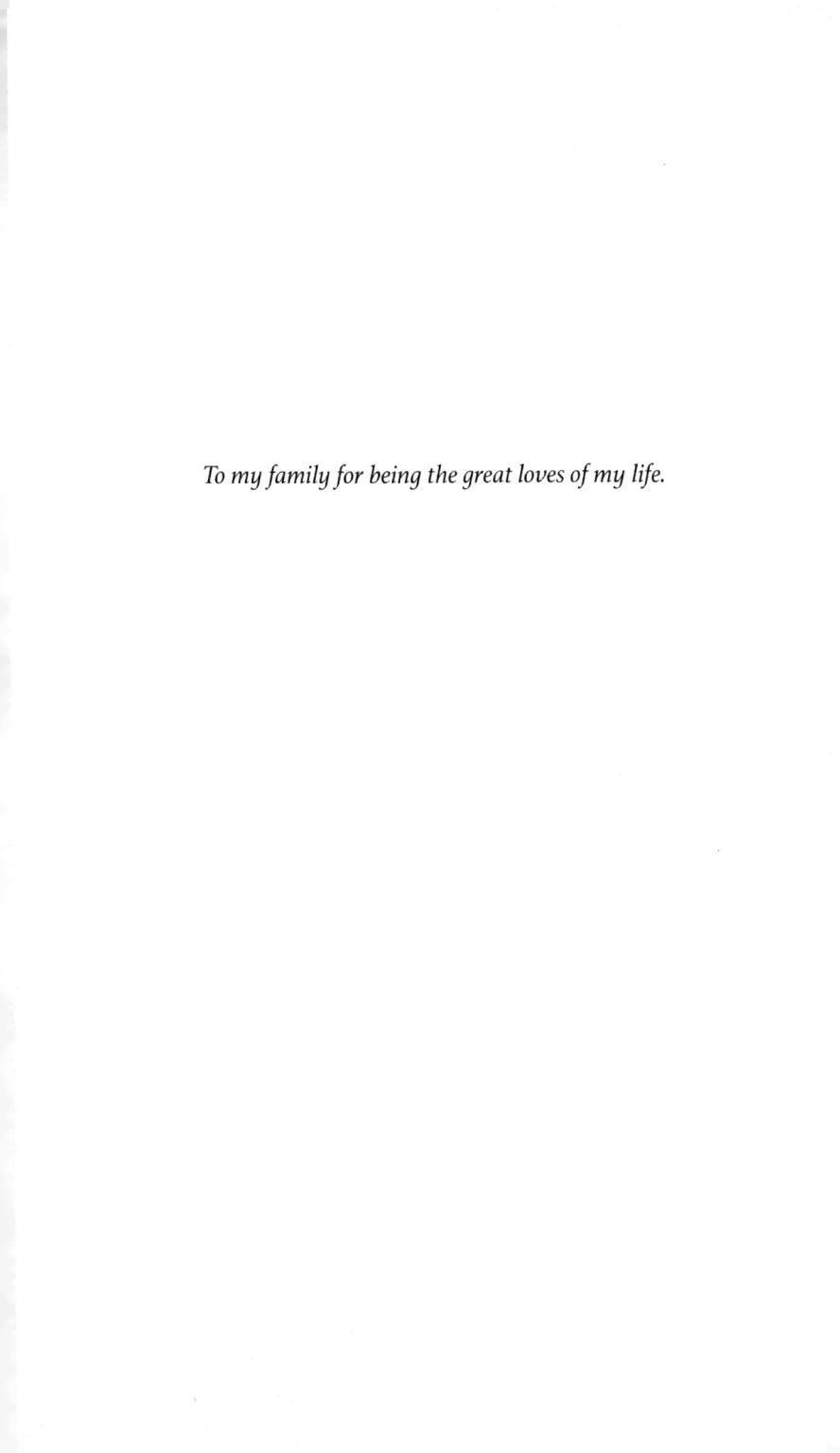

# 1

Rafe tapped the toe of his boot on the concrete floor of The Diner, located off the highway leading toward Lone Star Pass, Texas. He was halfway between home and Austin, in a small town on a main street. This was the first face-to-face meeting with the surrogate. And he was nervous as hell.

A tall woman walked in with long chestnut hair that reminded him of a person from the movies. He thought long and hard for a second and came up with the name: Jennifer Lawrence. Her eyes were a shade of blue he'd never seen before, like the sky on a clear spring day. She wore a serious expression on an oval face with near-perfect symmetry.

He stood up as she glanced around the diner. Her gaze found his, and for a split second his heart stopped beating. Chalking it up to nerves, he waved her over.

"Rafe," she said after making the short trip to his table. There were only half a dozen full tables at this hour of the afternoon. Three o'clock was sandwiched in right between lunch and dinner.

He took the outstretched hand, forcing his gaze away

from the basketball-sized lump in her belly. An unfamiliar feeling settled over him at seeing the pregnancy in person as opposed to over an app on the internet. In roughly five weeks, he was going to be a father. A half dozen campfires lit inside him at the thought of holding his and Emile's baby in a matter of weeks. Considering the odds against this day ever materializing, he'd gotten his miracle.

"Please, sit down," he said to Odette before pulling out the chair for her. The second her hand left his, another sensation engulfed him. This time, his hand was cold without her touch.

His overwrought nerves were getting the best of him, causing him to imagine things. Seeing this woman pregnant with his baby and Emile's legacy caused a knot to form in the center of his chest. One big enough to make something as simple as taking a breath hurt. It was moments like these he missed Emile the most. It should be her carrying the child. It should be her rubbing her growing belly. It should be her holding their child in her arms in a few weeks. A familiar anger surfaced. One that reminded him of everything he'd lost.

Odette took a seat and then scooted up as much as she could under the circumstances.

"I can't thank you enough for everything you're doing," he said, reclaiming his spot across from her at the square table.

"It's a business arrangement, pure and simple," she said as she crossed her arms over her chest and rested them on top of the bump. "Like I said when we first agreed I was the right person for the job, I'm a first-generation college student who bit off more than I can chew in student loans, despite finishing my degree in three years. Turns out, everyone was right. A liberal arts degree doesn't open a whole lot of doors in the corporate world."

Rafe resists the urge to press for answers even though he suspected there was more to the story. It might have been months ago, but he was almost certain she'd used those *exact* words back when he first interviewed her. They sounded stiff and rehearsed rolling off her tongue now. A sign she was lying? He couldn't imagine why she would lie about something so basic, unless she was running away from something or someone. Was there an abusive spouse in the background? No, a spouse would have come up in the background check and that would have raised a red flag. The agency sealed the records at her request to protect her privacy, but they'd done a thorough investigation along with drug and alcohol testing. The main tidbit about her personal life that had been shared was the fact Odette wasn't married, which didn't rule out an abusive boyfriend.

His hands fisted before he realized what he was doing. Forcing his fingers to relax, he picked up a menu. "Hungry?"

Odette's laugh was damn near musical. "Always."

"Order whatever you like," he said, checking out the apple cobbler a la mode. He'd already had lunch and it was too early for dinner.

"I'm pretty certain I eat my own weight every day at this point," Odette said as she grabbed a menu. "I've never weighed so much or eaten as often in my life." She caught herself being casual and sat up a little straighter. She cleared her throat—another sign she believed she'd said too much—and studied the plastic covered menu items. "Have you been here before?"

"A couple of times," he admitted, doing his best to radiate calm. He hoped she could relax a little in person, since she'd been standoffish during their brief check-in meetings. The first had come on the heels of success in the first trimester. The second had happened two months later and then it was one-per-month after that.

"What do you recommend?" she asked, perusing the list. Her eyebrows creased like she was taking a final exam.

"You can't go wrong with the BBQ Burger," he pointed out. "Definitely order the fries if you do. They're crisp." Another idea hit him as he looked over the menu. "The chicken fried steak shouldn't be missed, loaded with gravy, of course."

Odette laughed and he realized she was staring at him. He looked up, unprepared for the onslaught when their eyes touched.

"What did I say wrong?" he asked, hearing the gruff quality to his own voice.

"Nothing," she said quickly shifting her gaze. "Thank you for not telling me to eat a veggie burger or salad."

"I trust you're taking good care of yourself," he said like it was no big deal. He did trust her. He had to considering she was carrying the most precious thing he could ever hope to have, Emile's child. "Giving into a craving or two won't hurt anything."

"You're a classic enabler," she quipped, breaking some of the tension between them. It had been thick so far.

"Guilty," he said with a small smile. "But I believe in balance."

"Good point," she said. "Chicken fried steak it is."

A waitress walked up and introduced herself as Maddy. She looked to be in her early- to mid-twenties. "What'll you have?"

"May I?" Rafe asked as he glanced up at Odette.

"Be my guest," she said before handing over the menu and folding her arms across her chest again.

"The lady will have chicken fried steak, extra gravy—"

"On the side, please," Odette interjected.

Rafe nodded.

"On the side," he repeated before adding fried okra and mashed potatoes to the order. "I'll have apple cobbler a la mode and coffee, black."

"Milk for me," Odette said, sounding satisfied. "Of course, this sounds like a quick trip to heartburn city, but if the smells coming from the kitchen are any indication, it'll be worth it."

So far, a conversation about food was going fine. Could Rafe parlay it into something deeper? He wanted to get to know the person carrying his child a little better than what he'd read in her file. Asking direct questions might be pushing it though. She'd been tightlipped about her background, other than open access to medical exams and academic reports. Her privacy was important, which he understood since he'd guarded his as well. Being a Firebrand could make him a target. His family owned a successful cattle ranch, along with mineral rights to half a million acres of land. Most everyone in Texas and neighboring states had heard of his family name. Nondisclosure agreements had been signed, sealed, and delivered.

Maddy read the order from her notepad, confirming their choices. When they both nodded, she excused herself to get the drinks. Considering there wasn't a whole lot of business, she was back with coffee and milk on her tray before Rafe and Odette picked up on their talk.

"Holler if y'all need anything else," Maddy said. She had on a white button-down that was tied off at the waist, shorts, and boots. The standard waitress uniform let folks know they were deep in Texas.

"Will do," he replied before turning his attention toward

Odette. She was beautiful by most standards. He wouldn't argue. From what he knew of her personality, she was a good person. She was being guarded with him. Then again, these were unfamiliar circumstances to them both according to the file.

She sat back and studied him. "Mind if I ask a question?"

"Shoot," he said, figuring she might open up a little if he gave her a little information about himself. After all, he'd requested the two live together during her final month of pregnancy and she hadn't given her final answer yet. It only seemed right to know more than the basics about each other, if they were possibly going to live under the same roof at some point soon.

What else was it about Odette that drew him in and made him want to know more about her?

ODETTE BARNES SAT BACK in her chair, arms folded. The baby was active, and she was trying not to give that away in case Rafe asked to feel the movement. Her facial expressions could be like a billboard, or so she'd been told, and strangers asking to touch her belly creeped her out. Technically, the man wasn't an outsider since the baby belonged to him but still. This whole surrogacy was new territory and she was feeling her way through it best as she could.

Rafe Firebrand was unnervingly handsome in person. He had the kind of charisma that didn't necessarily translate over the internet, despite her believing him to be quite handsome there too. Plus, her connection was bad and they kept cutting out during several of their conversations. In the flesh, he had an almost animal-like magnetism that drew her in and made her want to stare. Refocusing on her glass of milk, she picked it up and took a sip.

Right now, she wanted to know why a surrogate. "My question might be sensitive, so you don't have to answer."

"Now, I'm even more curious," he admitted. "What's on your mind?"

She didn't want to offend the man in the first twenty minutes of their meetup. Besides, she needed to find a way to wiggle out of their agreement for her to live with him in the final weeks of the pregnancy. She'd been so desperate for the huge payout that she'd skipped right over that part of the agreement she'd signed. "I'm curious about what happened to your wife."

His face turned almost bleached-sheet white with the question.

She put her hands up, palms out, to stop him from answering. "Don't worry about it. That's none of my business." She'd clearly stepped on a landmine. "You don't have to say anything."

Rafe took a sip of coffee before turning his head to the side and looking out the window. When his hazel eyes had been intent on her, it was like her body came to life. Sensations battled for the upper hand, and she felt like something other than a desperate woman doing her best to find a solution to an almost impossible situation in her personal life. Since an attraction was out of the question, she dismissed her feelings as overwrought hormones.

"Let's see," he finally said after running his hand on the day-old stubble on his chin. His hair was dark, not quite as black as the coffee in his cup. More like espresso brown, which made his eyes stand out that much more. He had perfectly straight, white teeth when he'd smiled earlier that would make an orthodontist proud. A small scar, not more than half an inch, over his left eye gave him a rugged outdoorsy look that was almost irresistible. She had to will her hand to stay put so it wouldn't reach out to run her finger along it. "Her name was Emile."

She picked up on the use of past tense, bringing a hand up to cover her gasp. "I'm so sorry." She shook her head as a tear escaped. "I had no idea."

"Why would you?" he asked, but the question was rhetorical. "The information wasn't in the file."

"Can I ask why you're telling me now?"

"Because you should probably know more if you're going to stay under my roof and be in my care," he said.

Odette involuntarily shivered. Being in *someone's care* was foreign at best. She had no interest in relying on anyone other than herself. Besides, she'd been doing a good job so far.

"Did I say something to offend you?" he asked, his eyebrow quirked and the scar moved right along with it.

"No," she said. "It's just that I don't need someone to take care of me. I do well enough on my own."

"Oh, right," he said, still sounding a little confused by her reaction. He scratched his head. "I just thought, based on what I've read, these last few weeks can be...*tough*. I'd be happy to bring you water or milk..." He motioned toward her glass. "Whatever you need."

"I'm just...I don't..."

She was struggling to find the right words.

"It's just been me for a long time," she finally got out, the words feeling dry, even as they left her mouth. "I'm used to getting my own water...and milk. It would be weird for someone else to do that for me at this point." At thirty-two, she was too set in her ways to change. Plus, what good would it do to get used to someone being around, helping?

Especially when all that would change the minute the kid was born.

"Understood," Rafe quickly added with a hand gesture. "Believe it or not, I wasn't trying to offend you in any way or make your life difficult."

"No. Of course not," she defended. "I just wouldn't want to get too comfortable. That's all. It would be best if I kept my distance."

Strange enough, when she managed to lift her gaze to meet his, she was certain he understood.

"In fact, does anyone else know about the pregnancy? About me being the surrogate?" she asked before being interrupted by the waitress. His blank stare told her that she wasn't the only one keeping secrets.

Maddy brought over a tray with several plates. "Sorry about not asking if you wanted bread first."

"Not a problem," Odette reassured as she picked up the paper-wrapped utensils. "Bread with my meal works for me."

"Oh, good," Maddy said, as she set the plates down.

Odette could have sworn the young woman batted her eyelashes at Rafe, which riled her up. This waitress had no idea if Odette and Rafe were a couple. And, to make matters worse, Odette was pregnant.

"Babe, would you mind handing me the ketchup?" Odette asked Rafe. She shouldn't have done it, but the waitress was irritating.

"Holler if you want something else," Maddy said, her words directed at him. The waitress threw a cold shoulder in Odette's direction that almost made her laugh.

"Honey?" he asked, diverting to Odette. His dry crack of a smile reassured her that he had a sense of humor. It was strange that she wanted to know the baby would be in good hands, considering she had no rights to the child whatsoever. It was best to keep it that way too. She had her hands full in life as it was without adding a newborn to the equation.

"I'm good, babe," Odette said before reaching across the table to take the bottle he'd picked up.

"I'm needed in the kitchen." Maddy's smile faded before she excused herself.

"I'll bet you are," Odette mumbled.

As soon as Maddy was out of earshot, Rafe busted out laughing.

"Sorry," Odette said. "I had no right to do that, except the waitress was being rude. How does she know this baby isn't yours…? Well…I guess it is technically yours, but it could be *ours*. She doesn't know our situation or whether or not her flirting with you would be offensive to me. Women shouldn't do that to each other." She made a tsk-tsk noise while shaking her head.

"I caught her checking for wedding bands when she first came to the table," he admitted, looking just as offended. "Still didn't figure she would act on the lack of them because…well…it isn't difficult to see how pregnant you are."

"Right? So rude," Odette said, picking up her knife and fork before digging in and doing her best to shake off the disrespect. After the first bite, she gave a little hum of pure happiness that seemed to get Rafe's attention. Or did she have gravy on her face somewhere? She glanced up at him before catching his stare. "What?"

He opened his mouth before clamping it shut, like he had something to say but decided against it. What was that about?

Before she could ask, he cleared his throat. "What do you think?"

"About?" She didn't dare make any assumptions.

His eyebrow shot up. "The food."

"Good," was all she managed to say in response. Since they'd clearly moved on from the previous conversation, she had other pressing questions. Was he ready to provide answers?

## 2

"Is your family excited about the baby?"

Rafe shifted his weight, leaning back in his seat. How did he tell Odette the subject was sensitive, and he still hadn't found a way to work the announcement into conversation? "During the first trimester, the OB said most folks keep the news to themselves. I didn't want to jinx anything, considering this is already a miracle."

Odette set her fork down as she listened, chewing on another bite of the fried meal as she studied him. She nodded. "We've been in the clear for months now."

"Yes," he admitted. "But when I first decided to move forward, I knew the chances of a viable fetus being created was slim to none. Those eggs were all I had left of Emile, and I couldn't give the order to destroy them when she'd wanted them so badly. I thought, 'What the hell?' Why not go for it and let nature decide? I didn't want to say anything to my family because, honestly, I wasn't sure how they'd react. We've been through a lot recently."

A look of concern crossed her features. When it came to Odette, she was easy to read. Her face gave away what she was thinking. "What about Emile's family? Surely you've said something to them."

"I believe this child is a miracle and is meant to be," he said. "However, mentioning it to the future grandparents might bring up memories of their daughter. I didn't want to do that to them until I was certain there was a child to show."

"Sounds like a dangerous plan, if you ask me," she quipped.

"I'm just minimizing damage in the event there's nothing to talk about," he defended. Odette caught him off guard with her honesty.

The door opened as she continued eating, and he was shocked to see Morgan walk in. His brother glanced around the room before his gaze landed on Rafe. What *was* he doing here?

"I'd appreciate your discretion," Rafe said before waving his brother over.

Odette looked confused. "I would never reach out to your—"

"Morgan," Rafe interrupted as his brother approached the table. Rafe pushed to standing and then brought his younger brother into a bear hug. He'd always been able to tell the twins apart. They might look physically identical, but they dressed different and carried themselves in a whole different manner. Morgan was t-shirts and jeans, whereas Nick wouldn't be caught dead in a t-shirt. He wore western shirts and lived in a Stetson, whereas a backward facing ball cap was more to Morgan's taste. Today was no different. His brother was sporting a black baseball cap turned backwards with the bright orange family ranch logo on it.

His brother glanced at Odette. Right. Introductions.

"I'd like you to meet a supplier," Rafe halfheartedly said. He wasn't ready to introduce her to the family yet.

"Odette," she said, as she offered a handshake and a smile so warm that it could light a Christmas tree.

"Morgan," his brother said, but you probably already heard.

"Nice to meet you," she said, shifting her gaze to Rafe like she expected him to spill the details.

He wasn't ready to. Did that make him a jerk in her eyes?

"Wh-wh-what are you doing all the way out here, brother?" Rafe asked, throwing a playful punch that landed on Morgan's shoulder to deflect from his stuttering. It was a nervous habit he'd picked up as a teenager that, much to his annoyance, had stuck around. Of course, he didn't make a habit of putting himself in positions to cover a secret, so it didn't surface a whole lot.

His brother paused before responding, like he expected more of an explanation too. Odette leaned back in her chair and crossed her arms over her chest, resting them on her baby bump.

"Stopping through on my way home," Morgan said. "I pit-stopped for gas and called in a to-go order."

Relief washed over Rafe that his brother wasn't staying to eat. He had no plans to ask Morgan to join them. Awkward didn't begin to describe the sudden tension in the room.

"Don't let me stop you from eating while your food's warm," Morgan said, as he scanned the open kitchen area. "My order should be up, so I'll be on my way."

Clearly, his brother's radar was up. But Rafe wasn't ready to start making announcements yet. Tell one Firebrand and news would spread like wildfire despite anyone's best efforts to control the blaze.

Besides, Rafe had a bad feeling in the pit of his stomach, just like the one he'd had when he went to the oncologist's office with Emile. She'd been certain they were going to receive good news, but the cancer had spread. That had been the visit where they found out the current treatment plan wasn't doing its job. The memory of that day still gutted him.

Then again, the ominous feeling appeared on the regular now. Rafe expected bad news out of everything, which was part of the shock he'd felt when the pregnancy turned out to be viable.

And, yes, months had passed without him uttering a word to his family or Emile's. What was wrong with that? Did it mean he was being dishonest? Withholding information wasn't the same as lying...was it?

"What were you saying earlier about not wanting to jinx the news as the reason for not telling your family?" Odette asked, not lifting her gaze to meet his.

"I come from a large family," he explained. "If I tell one person, it's like telling everyone, despite the best intentions of keeping a secret. I plan on delivering the news in person to the whole family, if I can get everyone together. Or at least most of them."

"Sounds like a solid plan," she said with no conviction in her voice. Rafe was having a hard time figuring her out. Sure, her dislike for something played out on her features in the moment, but he didn't know her well enough to truly read her mind. Was she disappointed he hadn't told Morgan the baby she was carrying belonged to Rafe and was a Firebrand?

An admission like that would garner a whole lot of other questions he wasn't ready to tackle. Besides, there was something about the secret that kept it sacred somehow.

Like this news belonged to him for now. Growing up in a family of nine boys with nine cousins, also boys, it seemed like everything anyone did was fair game for gossip. The town treated Firebrands like tabloid fodder rather than human beings. Everyone wanted to rub elbows with the cattle ranching heirs and chew on all the gossip. Considering the family was large and divided, there'd been plenty of gossip to go around.

Still, looking at Odette and seeing the disappointment in her face made him feel like he was hiding something, rather than holding onto it until the time was right to share.

Guilt was a waste of time. So, why was he suddenly consumed with it?

By the time he picked up his fork and dug into his apple cobbler, the ice cream was a puddle.

"See you back at home, later?" Morgan asked as he stopped by the table on his way to the door.

"I'll be in Austin for a while," Rafe explained before holding up his cell. "If you or anyone needs me, I'll have this on at all times."

Morgan saluted before saying goodbye to Odette. Clearly, his brother's radar was up. The fact his gaze lingered on her belly didn't bode well. Then again, he'd never been a good liar. And had no intentions of starting now. He'd been honest earlier. The right timing hadn't come to deliver baby news—news he wasn't certain would be a reality. The odds had been stacked against this baby from day one. And yet, here they were in the final stretch. Rafe was about to become a first-time father.

Ready or not, a baby was due to arrive in a matter of weeks.

What had seemed like a good idea was beginning to freak him out. His breathing was suddenly panicky, his throat dry, and his palms damp. Was he prepared to care for a little one all on his own without Emile? Was it fair to bring a baby into the world who would never meet his or her mother? Who would grow up without knowing what it was like to have a female role model around? Because he'd all but given up on finding anyone he could care for as much as Emile.

What had he done?

This seemed like a good time to remind himself that he'd left the baby decision up to fate, and fate had answered with a healthy pregnancy so far. He set down his fork and studied Odette.

"You don't have to answer this question, but the only reason someone would go through nine months of pregnancy to hand over the child to someone must be for the money," he started.

"Your offer was very generous," Odette said without looking up. She did that a lot when she didn't like where a conversation was headed.

ODETTE DIDN'T WANT to go into her personal reasons for taking the half-a-million dollar offering, payable in installments as the pregnancy progressed. Producing a healthy child unlocked quarter of a million. More than enough money for a fresh start with her little sister. "Like I said, I'm behind on student loans and needed a way out. I'm young, physically fit, and the ad caught my eye. I could never make this kind of cash working at an office in such a short time."

Rafe's eyebrow shot up and she couldn't tear her gaze away from the scar and how it formed a small arch too. Almost like an echo.

Did he believe her?

So far, the conversation had been centered around Rafe and his family. Being the one in the hot seat with a question she wasn't comfortable answering made her feel like a spotlight was bearing down on her. It suddenly felt hot in the diner despite the cool temperatures outside. She swallowed and had to breathe slowly, so that she didn't give away her discomfort. That was hard enough in normal circumstances, but with Rafe Firebrand's gaze firmly upon her face...

He had squirmed in his chair earlier. Now it was her turn.

"The offer is substantial because I wanted this to be a job someone would be rewarded for, especially if the pregnancy made it to full term," he explained after taking a sip of what had to be cold coffee by now. "Like I already said, the chances of being to this point were negligible. I wanted the person willing to try to be more than compensated for their efforts for being willing to try at all."

The offer spoke to his generosity. She now understood why it would be important to keep his wife's or girlfriend's or fiancée's memory alive. "You never said why you wanted to take the chance at all." She sized him up. "You're still young enough to find someone else and start a family together."

"I'm pushing forty," he said.

"No," she argued. "The file said thirty-seven and that's still time."

"She's been gone five years and no one has come close to holding a candle to her," he admitted, averting his gaze.

"Five years?" she parroted before she could rein in her shock. She shook her head. "Sorry. It's none of my business and you don't have to tell me any of this."

He didn't immediately respond.

"I'm just surprised considering how good-looking you are. You seem to have your life together," she said, thinking there was probably a long line of women who would jump at the chance to spend time with him. Maddy the waitress had made her intentions clear. There had to be a host of others.

Rafe cracked a smile. Good. Because for a second there, she was afraid she'd offended him with her assessment.

"Thanks for the compliments," he said as Maddy returned with a pot of coffee in her hand.

"Refill?" she asked.

"Yes," he said, motioning toward the mug.

Maddy complied. "Anything else I can get you folks?"

"No, thanks," Odette said as Rafe looked to her for an answer.

"Just the check, please," he said.

"Alright then. I'll be right back," Maddy said before walking away.

Rafe picked up the full cup and then took a long, slow sip. "It's a lot like this coffee here."

Odette must have shot him a look, because he asked her to bear with him for a minute.

"It's not bad," he said, his tongue darting across his bottom lip. "It's drinkable and delivers the caffeine jolt I'm looking for. All in all, it's a pretty standard blend."

"I'll take your word for it," Odette said. "I miss caffeine." Along with a few other things that didn't need spelling out, but her hormones made her crave at times.

"Would you want to spend the rest of your life drinking this..." He lifted his cup and held it out. "Because once you've had the best, you'll always compare it to this. And no one has measured up or even come close. That's fine for a cup of coffee. Wouldn't be fair to a person."

Odette nodded despite never having felt anything close to those feelings. Not one person had come into her life that she couldn't live without. In a way, she was jealous of Emile. As horrible as her death must have been, she'd been truly loved by someone. Who got that?

"I was lucky once," he said before taking a sip. "Lightning rarely strikes in the same place twice."

Those words nearly broke her heart for him. Was it worse to have experienced real love and lost it? Judging from the sad quality to those gorgeous hazel eyes of his, she couldn't help but wonder if love was worth it.

The man was charming and seemed above board, or she never would have agreed to do this. Odette had done her own investigating before accepting the job.

Rafe cleared his throat and a blankness came over his expression. A distance that wasn't there a few moments ago when he spoke about Emile.

Odette had never wished for that kind of love, never wanted or needed it. Becoming dependent on another human being sounded like the worst mistake. Besides, bad luck seemed to follow her. Bad luck and bad choices. Then again, maybe she was just born bad.

Either way, she was determined to secure enough money to get as far away from home as possible and start a new life. She'd technically lied about being from Chicago, so it felt hypocritical to call Rafe out earlier for not telling his brother the truth about her and the baby.

Although, to be fair, she had just come back from the Windy City. Being back in Texas, where she could be spotted, made her uneasy. The ominous feeling that had become a cloak around her shoulders far too long kept her from getting too comfortable around Rafe.

One thing was clear. The baby she carried...*his* baby...

was going to be well loved and cared for. Odette would get a paycheck large enough to be able to lay low for a long time before picking up on a new life. And nothing would be able to stop her from keeping her sister safe.

The roar of a truck engine behind her followed by the sound of glass shattering caused Odette to suck in a breath. Before she could release a scream, Rafe dove toward her.

## 3

Instinct took over the second Rafe saw the front end of a truck come flying through the front window of the diner. His quick reflexes kicked in and he dove toward Odette and pulled her out of the way in the nick of time. The truck's front tire grazed his boot. The words *close call* didn't begin to cover it.

He'd cushioned Odette's fall with his own body. Thankfully, she'd landed on her side and not her belly. Still, he was concerned for her and the baby.

But first, he had to neutralize the threat. Rolling onto his side to place her next to him as gently as possible, he followed up by hop-kipping to his standing. He stayed crouched low enough not to be seen by the driver of the old silver truck as he approached.

There was no sign of the driver attempting to brake. There'd been too many instances of a criminal doing something just like this, before coming out shooting.

Tension was thick in the air as time seemed to stand still.

Rafe half-expected the driver's side door to swing open or a gun barrel to poke through the intact window. The front end of the truck was messed up. Airbags had deployed.

Where was the driver? Rafe was close enough to pop his head up but saw nothing.

"No driver?" he said out loud. It was a rhetorical question.

A couple of folks popped their heads up.

"Is it safe to come out?" Maddy shouted from behind the counter leading to the kitchen.

"I think so," Rafe said, opening the unlocked driver's side door.

Slowly, folks emerged from underneath their tables. The small kitchen staff filed out from behind the counter along with Maddy and another waitress who had been working the other side of the room.

Eyes wide, Odette scooted farther away from the truck, from him. The fear in her expression made him want to ask what else was going on in her life. Most of the folks inside the diner looked to be in shock. Odette had the kind of fear that said she'd half expected something like this to happen or worse. He took note to ask her about it as he double-checked the vehicle to ensure no one had crawled under the floorboard.

On second glance, no airbags had deployed. He'd assumed they had but that wasn't the case, indicating there'd been no weight in either seat.

A purse wedged on top of the gas pedal must have caused the vehicle to accelerate. An accident? The truck was old so it didn't have many of the current safety features that would prevent such an occurrence. It wasn't unusual in these parts for folks to leave key fobs inside vehicles on the floormat or keep the engine running if they were darting inside for a quick pick-up or errand.

Rafe cut off the engine to stop the carbon dioxide from poisoning the room, despite the gaping hole in the building. Glass crunched underneath his boots as he moved around to the back of the truck.

"Is anyone injured?" he asked, stopping at the newly made doorway leading outside to the parking lot.

There were a few mumblings, but the general consensus seemed to be that no one had been struck. Scared and shocked, maybe, but not injured other than scrapes and bruises from getting out of the way. Thank the stars for small miracles.

Sirens pierced the air as Rafe made his way outside. He glanced around as a couple stood behind their vehicle. A woman held onto a man with a look of horror stamped on both faces.

"We're all fine," he reassured, scanning the area.

An older woman came out of the store next door. She clutched her chest. A look of guilt crossed her features.

"Ma'am," Rafe started.

"I forgot my purse in my truck," the older woman said.

The couple came over to comfort her.

"It's okay, Margie," the woman said. She exchanged a look with Rafe that said there was a story. "You didn't do this on purpose."

Margie brought her hand up to cover her mouth. She had sun-worn skin and a full head of gray hair piled in a bun on top of her head. Glasses were attached to a fake pearl necklace that hung around her neck. She had on jeans, boots, and a flowery-print fleece sweatshirt.

"I could swear that I didn't leave my truck on this time," Margie said.

"Has this happened before?" Rafe asked.

The woman nodded. "She was inside the vehicle last

time. Didn't get the gearshift all the way in park before she reached into her purse. The truck lurched forward and smacked into a handicap parking sign."

Margie's cheeks turned three shades of red as a look of bewilderment crossed her features. "I could have sworn that I turned off the truck."

The woman put her arm around Margie, before looking over at Rafe. "I'm Deandra, by the way."

"Rafe," he said as the sirens neared.

"You need to listen to your son, Margie. It might be time to turn in your keys," Deandra said.

Margie conceded with a nod. "I just don't remember leaving my truck running."

Rafe didn't know Margie and he couldn't attest to her mental state. The thought of her losing her independence struck him, though. He felt sorry for her and could only imagine how awful it must be to turn over keys and have to depend on others.

"I'm sorry," Margie said, shaking her head. "I would never do anything like this on purpose."

"No one was hurt," he reassured. "Insurance will cover damage to the building, so you should be good there." Even if it didn't, he would offer to pay for repairs personally rather than watch this woman suffer any more than she already was. It was probably the fact he'd grown up with too many brothers and cousins, but he needed to make sure someone hadn't set Margie up. "Was there anyone else around when this happened?"

"I don't recall," Deandra said, clearly shaken up. "I wasn't really paying attention to everything going on around me. Benny and I were having a discussion and—"

"We were bickering about whose turn it was to decide what movie we were going to watch when we got home,"

Benny cut in. "And then...crunch. We heard the sound of the truck accelerate."

Their vehicle was parked facing the opposite direction of The Diner, so it would have taken at least a few seconds for them to get their bearings and turn around to check on the source of the noise.

A law enforcement vehicle marked *deputy* came roaring up. A man in his late thirties or early forties came out of the driver's side after stopping in the middle of the lot.

"Deputy Marsden," he said as he assessed the area. "Is anyone injured?"

"No, sir," Benny interjected.

"Who witnessed the accident?" Deputy Marsden asked the small crowd that had gathered.

It seemed a little premature to classify this as an accident, despite the older lady with a bad memory being all too ready to take the blame.

Rafe didn't like this one bit. He'd had a creepy feeling earlier and now this. He couldn't quite put his finger on why. Was someone trying to get revenge on his mother? The family had been receiving threats ever since her arrest. His brother Vaughn had been through hell and back. Was it time to call a family meeting to discuss this? Or was this purely an accident? Wrong place, wrong time on his part?

ODETTE'S STRESS levels were through the roof. The baby had stilled, which she didn't take as a good sign. Was the little person in stress overload? A cramp nearly doubled her over as she sat with her back against the legs of a chair for support. She winced and sucked in a breath.

"Are you alright, dear?" a sweet older woman asked as she crossed the room to get to Odette.

"I will be," she responded. "In a minute."

Maddy brought over a glass of water. "Here. Drink this. It might help."

She was willing to try just about anything and, besides, it would give her something to do. "Thank you." She took the offering and sipped, waiting for word of what happened to cause the truck to make a new doorway. Fear enveloped her and she had a creepy feeling about this.

"Any idea what's going on out there?" the older woman asked Maddy.

"No, but I'll go check," Maddy promised. "Hold tight."

As she took off toward the small crowd that had gathered outside, Odette took in a few slow, deep breaths. The fear this could have been a pointed attack tried to take hold. She'd read about these kinds of situations in the news, but experiencing it was a whole different ballgame. Another fear crept in. *He'd* found her.

No. No. Impossible.

Odette couldn't allow herself to go there. She'd been careful so far despite returning to the same state where he lived. She was close to Austin, not Houston where he lived and worked. He couldn't possibly have tracked her movements here.

Could he?

Before she could get too far down that path, Rafe came back inside and made a beeline to her.

"There's an older lady who seems to have left her handbag inside her vehicle," he explained. "The deputy is coming in to take statements, but I wanted you to know what happened first."

Odette studied him as his tongue darted across his

bottom lip. He wasn't lying. There was no reason. Then, it dawned on her what was happening. He didn't believe the story.

"Is she alright?" she asked, worried about the elderly person involved.

"She's fine," he reassured. "Standing out there, talking to law enforcement. To be fair, she's a little disoriented as to how this could have happened when she felt like she was being so careful."

"So, this has happened before?" Odette asked.

"Something like this, but not nearly to this scale," he continued.

It did seem odd that a purse could do this kind of damage since the vehicle would have had to slip out of gear. She scanned the onlookers that had gathered, searching for him as fear gripped her.

"It's a good thing Margie wasn't inside when that thing rammed through," the older woman said as she pushed up to standing. "They'll have to take her license away for this one."

Odette probably shouldn't feel bad for the older woman under the circumstances. If this really was her doing, she shouldn't be behind the wheel. And yet, she felt a well of sympathy anyway. She understood what it was like to feel like your life was out of your own control.

"Let's get you in a chair," Rafe said as she realized he was studying her. "You can't be comfortable sitting on the hard flooring."

"I didn't think about it, but a chair would be nice," she said, taking the hand he was offering. The instant their skin touched, electricity pulsed at the point of contact. She cleared her throat and stood up, letting go as quickly as possible.

Rafe brought over a chair where she sat for the next hour while folks gave their statements, including her.

"Is there any possibility this might not be the older woman's fault?" she asked the deputy after he cleared her to leave the scene.

He shook his head. "I'm not finished with the investigation yet, but the evidence supports Margie being at fault."

Odette nodded as Rafe offered an arm, and then walked her outside to her vehicle. It was a small luxury to have a used car to drive around. One she could afford to pay cash for with the down payment Rafe had given her on the surrogacy.

"I'd like to finish this conversation at my apartment," he said to her.

"You have an apartment near here?" she asked, surprised.

"I rented one to be close to the hospital," he said. "Just like the contract said."

"About that..." she hedged.

"Is there a problem with living under the same roof during these last few weeks before the birth?" he asked. "Because there wasn't one when we signed the agreement."

Odette couldn't argue there. She didn't have a leg to stand on. She'd signed the document, enamored with the amount of money she was about to receive. Living in the same apartment didn't seem like it would be much of a problem months ago.

Now?

She wasn't so sure she wanted to be close to Rafe during these last few weeks. "It just seems personal to share space and I've been wondering if we could talk it through, to see if it still makes sense."

"You want to do that right here and now?" he asked. His

eyebrows drew together when he was disappointed, like now. His hazel eyes seemed to grow an even more concentrated shade. And he came across as even more intense.

The man was tall. She'd noticed it before but standing next to him made it blindingly obvious he was well over six feet tall. Six-foot-three or four if she had to venture a guess. At five-feet-seven-inches, she wasn't exactly short but he practically towered over her. And yet, she didn't feel intimidated in the least by his strong physical presence.

It could stem from the fact he'd literally just saved her life.

"Thank you, by the way," she said realizing she hadn't done so already. He might have made the heroic dive to save his baby and not her, but she benefited and appreciated him for it anyway.

"We should probably swing by the hospital," he said to her. "Just to be safe."

Another cramp nearly doubled her over. She fought against the dark cloud feeling that made it feel like her plan was fragile and could fall apart at any moment. She received the lion's share of the money for a successful pregnancy here at the end. She couldn't afford to lose everything now. Not when she was so close.

And yet something else threatened to break her if this pregnancy didn't pan out. For one, it was impossible not to grow close to a baby growing inside her. Then there was Rafe. After meeting him, knowing this child was all he had left of the woman he'd given his heart to, Odette wanted to give him this more than anything.

Was she falling down a rabbit hole when it came to Rafe Firebrand? More importantly, could she pull herself back out on her own?

# 4

"Are you okay?" Rafe asked, realizing it was a foolish question. There was no way she was okay after nearly being rammed with a truck coming through a window. "Don't answer that."

Odette gave a look of appreciation. He could only imagine what was going on in her mind right now.

"Do you want to come with me, instead of driving?" he asked.

"I hate to leave my car here," she conceded. "But with these cramps, it's probably best all round if I don't get behind the wheel."

"A tow service can bring your vehicle to my apartment. It could be there by the time you're checked out by a doctor," he offered, trying to sweeten the deal. The thought of her driving when he saw how unexpected the pain came on and how intense it was, gave him heartburn.

Odette stood there for a long moment, her gaze unfocused like she was looking inside herself for the right answer. She bit down on her bottom lip, then said, "Okay."

Rafe didn't look a gift horse in the mouth. He fished out

his phone, located a tow service, and made the call before she could change her mind. This felt like progress and he'd take it. Sure, he wanted everything to be fine with the baby. That was a given. More and more, he realized Odette's well-being was just as important and not because she was carrying his kid. Because she was a kind, decent person who was in some kind of bind. Otherwise, she wouldn't have taken on the surrogacy. Could he talk her into discussing the real reason?

It was a long shot, but he wanted to know more about her and what made her tick. He chalked his interest up to wanting to get to know the woman who was carrying his child. It sounded strange when he thought about the situation like that. Don't get him wrong, he appreciated her for all she was doing. Seeing her in person, seeing her pain when she had cramps, made him realize just how much her body had likely gone through in the pregnancy. He was also beginning to see how fragile it could be, and how her body was as fragile as the baby she carried. *His baby.*

The thought of holding his child in his arms nearly knocked him back a step. He never thought this day would come after Emile…

The fact she wouldn't be here to see what they'd created together from not much more than their love for each other was harder than he realized. Then again, this was all new territory for him. Rafe had no idea what he'd been getting into and felt way in over his head to be honest. But he was going with the flow and trying to make the best of the opportunities being presented to him. He'd made the decision on pure emotion, pushing logic aside, which wasn't something he normally did. He could only hope he'd made the right calls so far.

Once they were cleared at the hospital, and that was the

only outcome he could allow himself to believe, he could convince her to stick around his Austin apartment.

After the arrangements were made for her car to be towed, he held out an arm. "Ready?"

She nodded, taking the offering. He was slowly getting used to the jolt of electricity that came with contact. It was becoming oddly reassuring in ways he didn't want to examine.

The main reason he wanted to know more about Odette had to do with her carrying his baby. Emile's baby. It was natural to want to understand a person in her position.

No more cramps hit on the walk to his truck. None came on the way to the hospital either. He chose the one closest to his apartment so she could get used to it. This was going to be the place where she gave birth. His attorney had offered a document detailing ways in which to make the surrogate feel the most relaxed. Getting to know her environment before the delivery was one of them. It was also the reason he wanted her to agree to stay at his place. He wasn't trying to keep an eye on her in case she slipped in a glass of wine or a smoke; both were forbidden in the legal documents, and he didn't doubt her intention of following those instructions. Rafe wanted to make sure that she was calm and had everything she might need to get through those last few weeks, which he'd been warned could be the most uncomfortable and difficult.

The lawyer had warned Rafe of all the pitfalls of using a surrogate. Surrogacy could be emotionally and physically draining. Hormones heightened emotions and a surrogate could have doubts about her choice as time went on. After meeting Odette, Rafe saw how committed she was to delivering a successful end result. With the physical demands, he could only imagine how ready she might be to cross the finish line so she could get her body back. With this being her first pregnancy, she had no idea how her body would react, despite being healthy and taking care of herself.

"How are you really?" Rafe finally asked as he navigated off the highway. He'd been lost in thought for most of the ride, as had Odette. There were times throughout a day like today that he needed to mentally power down so he could process.

"I'm struggling a little bit to be honest," she admitted. "But I'll get through to the other side."

"Do you want to talk about it?" he asked, hoping she trusted him enough to open up. "Other than the obvious fact, anyone would be shaken up after what just happened."

Odette released a slow breath.

"It freaked me out," she said. "But all I could think was that I hope the baby is okay."

From the corner of his eye, he saw her caress the bump in a protective motherly fashion.

"It's not about the money, either," she quickly added. "I've been hosting this tiny human for months now, feelings its every move and it's impossible not to be attached to it."

"Makes sense," he said.

"Which doesn't mean I feel like I have any claim," she said. "I know the deal and I'm doing my part but I didn't expect to..."

"Have such a strong emotional attachment?" he asked, finishing the sentence for her.

"Right," she said.

Rafe nodded. "I appreciate your honesty."

"It doesn't freak you out, does it?" she asked.

"Not at all," he clarified. "It makes me see you as a human being and not a machine who can pump out babies without the least thought of what happened next."

She laughed at the machine bit. Making her laugh was right up there with one of his favorite things today.

"Sorry if that sounded strange," he said, letting himself crack a smile.

"It didn't," she said. "In fact, it makes you seem more human too."

He could appreciate that. "You know the reason behind my decision to move forward with trying for a child."

"You're ready to be a father," she said.

"Partly," he admitted. "Can you ever truly be ready to be responsible for another human being? Plus, it's a lifelong commitment. I could never be one of those parents who brings up a kid until they graduate high school and then gives them the boot."

"I'd be shocked if you were, even after what little time we've spent together," she said.

Granted, they'd only been around each other for a few hours at this point, but it was enough to get a sense of a person. Working a ranch, hiring folks who were passing through town looking for work, he'd honed his skills at figuring people out. The eyes always gave the person's intentions away. The worst people had deadness in their gaze that was hard to explain, but easy to spot.

Rafe prided himself on being a good judge of character. He still had questions about Odette but he didn't doubt she was one of the good ones. Living together over the new few weeks would give him a chance to really get to know her.

∽

ODETTE WASN'T CONVINCED STAYING in Rafe's apartment was such a good idea for reasons she didn't want to overanalyze. She'd been an overthinker from birth, it seemed, so she resisted the urge to examine the real reason six ways past Tuesday.

"You ever want children?" he asked.

Odette was caught off guard by the turnaround. "Me?"

"Yes. You. Do you plan to have a family?" he continued.

"I don't think about it much," she said. "At least, not starting my own family. I have a half-sister…"

He nodded as he artfully navigated through the narrow car-lined streets of downtown Austin.

How much of her personal life should she share? How deep should she go into her background? "She's young and needs my help financially, so, I guess my main focus is making sure she's well cared for. Until she's safe…"

Odette slipped. She'd meant to say secure. Safe was a whole different connotation. One she'd been hoping to avoid discussing.

"How old is she?" he probed.

She shifted in her seat, rechecking her seatbelt to ensure it didn't cross over her belly in a weird place. "A lot younger than I am."

Silence in the cab stretched on for a long moment as she thought about seven-year-old Andie being tucked away in a boarding school. Her half-sister had put on a brave face. It was an expression no seven-year-old should have to wear.

Rafe seemed to get the hint this topic was off limits when he changed the subject. "What kind of work did you do before?"

"I ran a small online jewelry shop that I inherited from my mother," she said wistfully. "I lost her last year."

"I'm sorry," Rafe said with the kind of compassion that made her believe he meant those words. A man like him had honor and lived by a code. She didn't have to know every detail of his life to realize he was one of the good ones.

"Thank you," she said, realizing this was the first time she'd spoken to anyone about her mother's death. "It happened suddenly." She paused for a few moments. "I made promises."

It seemed they'd both lost someone they loved. Rafe's loss might have been five years ago, but his pain was still raw. Odette lost her mother last year and hadn't slowed down long enough since to process any of it. Getting her half-sister away from her jerk of a father had been Odette's only focus. At first, all she could think about was the *how*. Once the plan was in action, Odette was early in a pregnancy and sick.

"I'm certain you'll deliver on your word," he reassured. Again, his sentiment brought a sensation of warmth over her.

It was nice to finally be able to talk to someone about her mother. "I miss her."

"I can imagine," he said. "Sounds like the two of you were close."

"Like two peas in a pod, people used to say," Odette offered. "We used to get together at least once a week for a girls' night. My stepfather hated it." She clamped her mouth shut, not wanting to discuss him.

"Sounds like a jerk," Rafe said out of the blue.

He had no idea.

"What about you?" she asked, turning the tables. "Are you close with your parents?"

Rafe shook his head. "Can't say that I am. The family was split apart for most of my life. Too much testosterone and a grandfather who pitted his sons against each other far too long."

"Didn't you say the family is huge?" she asked, appreciating the fact he didn't protest to the change in topic.

"It is," he admitted with a smile that said he loved his family despite 'too much testosterone' as he'd claimed. "Like I mentioned, nine boys on each side all ranging in age from twenty-five to thirty-nine."

"I can't imagine feeding all those people," she said with a laugh, appreciating the lighter topic. "Especially hungry teenagers."

"We were a lot," he said with a laugh that warmed her heart. "Only recently have both sides of the family started to reconcile after a lifetime of working against each other. My grandfather is to blame. He was one ornery sonofabitch." He glanced over at her. "Excuse the language."

"Not a problem," she said.

"I'll have to get used to watching my tongue when the baby arrives," he said. He'd clearly been giving fatherhood a lot of thought, despite making the decision to move forward and attempt a pregnancy with zero expectations anything would come of it. Then again, he'd had more than half a year to adjust to the idea. "Can't have his or her first word be dammit or worse."

The smile he cracked could warm a city if the power went out on a cold February day.

"Can I ask why you didn't want to know the sex of the baby?" she continued, since he'd brought the baby into the conversation.

He shrugged. "If I had to guess, I'd say that I wanted to be surprised. It really doesn't matter to me one way or the other. I'm going to love the little sprig one way or the other. Guess I didn't think it was that important."

She wondered if some of it had to do with not wanting to become too attached to the kiddo before it was actually here. She couldn't blame him if that was the case. Anyone who'd suffered would probably feel the same.

There was an added pressure now, though, to ensure this kiddo made it into the world healthy. This was part of the reason she resisted the idea of living under the same roof. Seeing the disappointment on his face if something went wrong...

Odette couldn't let herself go there.

"Do you have a preference?" she asked.

"A boy would be nice. Having someone to throw a ball with or teach the ranching life to would be cool. Only if he was interested though. Cattle ranching is a commitment that not everyone is up for. I wouldn't judge him if it wasn't for him," he said. "Then again, having a daddy's little girl would be pretty amazing too."

"You really don't care, do you?" she asked.

"Not really," he said. "I do wonder about having a little girl running around with her mother's eyes. Emile had the most honest shade of brown eyes I've ever seen."

The way he spoke about her caused Odette's heart to squeeze. She'd dated around, but could only imagine what it would be like to have someone talk about her with the same reverence with which he spoke about Emile.

It was silly to be jealous of a ghost. So, why was she?

Arriving at the hospital stopped conversation. Rafe walked over to her side of the truck after parking and offered an arm.

## 5

Relief washed over Rafe after a quick trip to the ER and a thumbs up from the attending physician. The detour only took an hour out of the afternoon and was well worth the time loss to gain reassurance everything was still on track with the baby.

"I thought you said this was an apartment," Odette said, jaw dropping, as he turned into the small complex and hit the button to open the security gate.

"It's more like a townhouse," he admitted. "I thought we could use the extra space to spread out so we're not tripping over each other. You can have a whole floor to yourself this way if you want it." The three-story came furnished and with art already on the walls. All it needed to make it feel like home would be a few personal touches.

Odette issued a grunt, and then quickly apologized for it.

"What's that all about?" he asked as he pulled into the oversized garage. He'd seen pictures of the place online. He'd arranged for some of his clothing to be brought here and there was a full closet with everything Odette might need in her room. He parked and then came around to her side of the vehicle to open the door.

"Nothing," she said.

He stared at her as he helped her out of the truck. "It sounded like something and if this...*arrangement* is going to work, we have to be able to communicate with each other and be honest."

The most beautiful pair of blue eyes blinked up at him as she placed a hand on her back like it ached. "You're right." She issued a sharp sigh. "I'm not trying to offend you but I didn't grow up around money and I'm not sure I'd ever be comfortable with the amount you and your family seem to have."

The subject of money had followed him for his entire life. His mother couldn't be satisfied with the amount they had. Look where that had gotten her.

"Okay," he said with dread in his voice that he thought he'd perfected hiding; at least until faced with Odette's honesty. Closing the door behind her, he fished out a door key. The Realtor had mailed it to the ranch along with a security code that would need to be reset at some point. The task jumped up the list after the restaurant scare. As he tapped the keypad to disarm the alarm, he continued. "I appreciate your honesty, so here goes. I didn't do anything to deserve the amount of money that I have in the bank. It's not as much as some folks believe it is, but it's nothing to sneeze at either. The reason I still have it is because I don't spend a whole lot." He shrugged. "I don't need much."

He unlocked and opened the door for her, before indicating she should go first. After the pair of them entered, he closed the door.

"Do you mind locking it?" she asked. This close, he could see dark circles underneath her eyes.

"Not at all," he said before doing just that.

"You do seem down to earth," she conceded before walking up a stairwell. She stopped midway, causing him to realize stairs might not be such a good idea for a late-term pregnant person.

"Ranchers, in my humble opinion, usually are," he pointed out, trying not to sound as defensive as he felt. Funny that he found himself defending his character to a near stranger. Odder still, this person he didn't know very well happened to be carrying his and Emile's child. Life sure knew how to throw curve balls at him.

At the top of the stairs, Odette stopped. "Wow. This place is beautiful."

"It's simple," he said, following right behind her. Instinct had him extending an arm behind her in case she lost her balance and tried to take a step back only to find air. With a hand close to her lower back, electricity sizzled in the space between them. Rafe wrote it off as his emotions getting the best of him. "But should have everything we need to get through the next few weeks." Her protest about staying here was churning in the back of his mind. Contract or no, he wouldn't push the issue. Of course, he wanted her in the townhouse so he could help during the final weeks—the doctor said getting across the finish line could require plenty of rest—but he'd respect whatever she needed.

"I'd say it does," she said, walking into the open concept kitchen, dining, and living room space. "It's so light and bright in here."

He nodded.

White cabinets in the kitchen along with marble countertops brightened up the room. Copper pots hung over the island that had several comfortable barstools pushed up against it, bringing a warm feeling to the room. This wasn't anything like his place back at the ranch, but he was considering redecorating that space. He'd planned to bring in an expert before the baby became mobile. Making any changes to his home before he talked about the child would bring too many questions, so he'd put plans on the back burner. To be honest, he was still in a state of mild shock that the pregnancy had made it this far. The dark cloud seemed to be thickening around him, over him, and the incident at the restaurant felt like a beginning instead of a one-off.

Telling his family the news before the baby was born seemed like an even worse idea now, almost as if such an action would jinx their luck so far.

"Make yourself comfortable," he said to Odette as he walked into the kitchen and checked the fridge. It was amazing what could be done with a phone these days. The fridge was stocked with pre-made meals, breakfast items, and drinks.

"The couch looks great. Mind if I put my feet up?" she asked.

"Go right ahead," he said. "You won't offend me."

Odette made a beeline across the room, slipped off the ballet flats she had on, and then made herself comfortable in the sofa-recliner. The color palette in the living room was warm, with a spot of color on the wall in the form of a blue painting on a white canvas. The blue resembled a brush stroke as though a painter had been too busy to finish. All the artist had time for was one perfect stroke.

"Can I bring you some water?" he asked, figuring she'd earned the right to put her feet up.

"Yes, please," she said, surprising him. He'd expected her to remind him that she was fully capable of getting her own water. Thankfully, she didn't seem ready to put up a fight and was at least a little resigned to accepting his help.

Under normal circumstances, he would spoil her rotten. Odette would be offended, though. He admired and respected her independent streak. His had always been a mile long. Emile, on the other hand, had been taken care of her entire life and had expectations. Granted, he hadn't minded at the time and wished like hell she was here to make demands now. But Odette was different. He didn't want to use the word stronger, but it applied.

Losing Emile to sickness had brought on the worst kind of pain. To be fair, there was no easy way to lose the love of his life. Emile had been warmth and sleeping in on Sundays. She'd been his comfort zone and safe space.

He filled a glass, forcing the memories back into the vault where they never saw the light of day. Odette's eyes were closed and her steady, even breathing told him she'd nodded off. He set the water down on the coffee table at almost the exact moment his cell buzzed in his pocket. Rather than risk waking her, he made a beeline for the staircase leading to the second floor before the call rolled into voicemail.

Halfway up the stairs, he fished out his phone and checked the screen. He answered a second later. "Hey, Morgan. Everything okay?"

"I was about to ask you the same question," Morgan responded. Having a concerned family was normally a good thing. Right now, they were an inconvenience.

"I'm good," he said quickly. Too quickly?

"Because if you weren't, I'd be here for you no matter what," Morgan continued.

Rafe didn't immediately speak.

"You seemed caught off guard earlier at the restaurant and were acting exactly like that time when we were kids, when you were trying to hide the fact you'd just sold my favorite baseball card to drum up enough cash to take Melissa Farmer out to the movies," Morgan continued.

"That was a long time ago," Rafe conceded.

"And yet here we are," Morgan said, lightening his tone. No doubt, he was trying to ease some of the tension on the line.

There was no way Rafe was ready to discuss Odette or Emile or the baby, but there was something else on his mind that he was comfortable talking about. "I'm worried about the situation with our mother."

"By situation, you mean the fact she's in jail facing attempted murder charges," Morgan said; his tone had a detachment quality to it that Rafe recognized as his brother's defense mechanism.

"Have you visited her?" Rafe asked, realizing just how much the topic had been weighing on the back of his mind now that he'd opened that can of worms. He couldn't say that he'd ever been particularly close with his mother, but that didn't mean he didn't appreciate her for bringing him into this world. Pregnancy looked to be hard and he had no idea how his mother had birthed nine children. Of course, the realist in him said she'd done it to win favor with a father-in-law who'd constantly pitted his only two sons against each other.

"No," Morgan admitted. "I have no idea what I'd say to her."

"I feel the same way," Rafe admitted as he turned around and sat down at the top of the stairs. "It's messed up."

"All I keep wondering is how she became so greedy," Morgan continued.

Rafe had thought along the same lines for years before this happened. "Money is only good when it's used to bring positive into a situation." He couldn't regret the amount of money he was paying Odette to carry his child. She deserved every penny and more, as far as he was concerned, after putting her body through all this and giving him a child.

The fact he was going to be a father smacked him square in the chest. He should be used to the idea by now. A voice in the back of his mind warned him not to get too attached to the idea either. The baby wasn't here yet. There'd been an incident at the restaurant that could have turned deadly if his reflexes weren't quick. Speaking of which, his brother would hear the news sooner or later, so he might as well spill.

"A truck ran through the diner, but no one was seriously hurt," Rafe said, changing the subject. He couldn't think or talk about their mother for long without the dark cloud sucking him under.

"What the hell?" Morgan asked. "I had no idea."

"That's why I'm telling you," he said. "I didn't want you to hear it on the news and be left wondering if I was okay. I'd planned to shoot a text once I got settled in Austin."

Morgan issued a sharp sigh. "Thank heaven you're all right. I don't know what I'd do if I lost another family member." A beat passed between them in total silence. "I didn't mean it the way that came across."

"I figured," Rafe said, letting his brother off the hook. Their family situation was one for the books. "We should probably have a family meeting at some point to discuss steps moving forward with our mother."

"Dad has it under control for now," Morgan said. "I think he's trying to protect us as best as he can."

Rafe was beginning to see there were no easy answers when it came to parenting. Kids didn't come with a rulebook or any type of instructions. Based on his own large family, he knew everyone was born with a certain personality. Nurture could only do so much against nature, in his opinion.

A scream sounded from downstairs.

"I have to go," Rafe said, already to his feet and taking two steps at a time. He ended the call with his brother before he hit the landing.

∽

ODETTE BLINKED her eyes open as she tried to calm her racing heart. Glancing around the strange room, she tried to get her bearings, pushing up to sitting on the unfamiliar couch.

"Hey, everything okay?" Rafe's voice shouldn't comfort her as much as it did.

She shifted her gaze to him as he bolted toward her, concern lines etched into his forehead. "Yes. Sorry." She managed to get out the words in between gasps for air. "Must still be freaked out from the incident earlier."

Odette wasn't a natural liar, so she hoped he didn't catch on. She had, however, become a little too good at covering her emotions. Her explanation was partially true. The vehicle coming through the window had stressed her out. She glanced down and realized she was cradling her bump.

Forcing a calm she didn't feel, she sat up a little straighter and then reached for the water. She didn't get far before Rafe was helping her. He extended a long arm to the coffee table and handed over the water. Their fingers brushed, and a jolt of electricity caused her to gasp.

"There's no need to apologize for being human," he said in the kind of masculine voice that sent sensual shivers skittering across her skin. Rafe had an effect on her like no other.

She took a sip of water to ease the sudden dryness in her throat.

"I'll stay here if you want to try to go back to sleep," he offered with a look of sincerity that said he wouldn't budge if it meant she could rest.

In all her years of dating, why hadn't she met anyone like Rafe Firebrand? He had honor and warmth in spades, not to mention sex-in-a-bucket good looks. The man was still deeply in love with a woman who'd been gone five years. He was having a child that she suspected he wasn't quite ready for out of extraneous and difficult circumstances. Gearing up for single parenthood despite not leaning on the large family he had back home.

There were so many questions she'd like to ask. Were they as off-limits as the man?

# 6

The sound Odette had made a few minutes ago must have scared Rafe beyond measure. Was it the thought of losing someone else that had kicked his adrenaline into high gear?

"I doubt I could sleep after being shocked awake," Odette admitted. Her flushed cheeks must be giving away her embarrassment about the outburst. It had been a day for the books.

"What can I get to make you more comfortable then?" he asked.

"As good as lunch was, all that fried food is making my mouth feel gross. A toothbrush would be nice. I swear I taste and smell things in a way that I never have before. Everything is amped up." She didn't even want to get started on how much her taste buds had changed, or the fact she'd never been a crier until all those hormones kicked in.

"Can I help you upstairs to the bathroom?" he asked in a voice that made her think he felt more helpless than she did.

"I would like that a lot actually," she said as she pushed

the button that made the seat return to normal. "But I can probably manage the stairs by myself. If you could just point me to the supplies, that would be amazing."

"Follow me," he said, holding out his arm. Taking the offering would be emotional suicide, so she opted to step in front of him instead after a quick smile. It might be foolish to refuse to touch him again or let him be her anchor, but she was in survival mode at this point. Being here would keep her flying underneath the radar in case Guy had caught up with her. She shuddered thinking about her stepfather. But that also reminded her that she needed to check on her half-sister. Would she be able to do that while staying here?

Rafe had his cell in hand. The minute they crested the stairs, he was head-down on the phone. Rather than ask him what he was doing, which was none of her business, she followed his direction into the master bedroom.

"I can't take this room," she protested.

"Why not?" he asked, sounding clueless.

"Because you paid for this place, for one," she quickly countered.

"And?"

The fact he stood there like the first reason didn't amount to a hill of beans shouldn't make her laugh. It did.

"It's simple math," she said. "You paid, so you should get the best bedroom."

"I won't sleep unless I know you're comfortable," he argued. "Plus, I don't want you walking up another set of stairs to the other bedrooms."

"This place has four floors?" she asked.

He nodded. "Three stories of living space."

"And are you telling me the master takes up an entire floor?" she asked, trying to absorb the fact.

"There's an office adjacent to it, but I had it set up as more of a lounge area for you, if that's okay," he said like it was nothing.

It would mean she wouldn't have to walk up more stairs if she didn't want to. "Can I check it out?"

"Sure thing," he said, stepping aside and holding out his arm like he was presenting a new car.

She took the steps down a small hallway before entering a room with the most comfortable looking loveseat along with a flatscreen and a small kitchenette in the corner. Could she go back to her normal life after staying here for a month? "This is all too much." She took a couple of steps backing away.

"Not really," he said. "I figured you might need to stick to one floor in the final week and I thought this would provide enough comfort to ease some of your suffering. The way I see it is you're doing the heavy lifting here. All I'm doing is providing as much comfort as possible in the final weeks. You've done all the work alone up to this point but I'd like to be here for you now."

"How do you know I'm alone?" she asked, wondering if he broke the agreement and dug into her personal life. Not that it would matter at this point. The point of no return had come and gone a while back. She was very pregnant and the baby was due in a matter of weeks. There was no turning back now.

"The fact you like to do things for yourself was my first clue," he said, catching her off guard with his response. "It's a lot like me. It seems we both have an independent streak a mile long."

Odette ducked out of the room and weaved her way into the master bathroom, rather than touch that statement. She didn't want to think about the ways in which her and Rafe were alike. Or think about the chemistry that sizzled between them. It was easier to chalk it up to hormones or imagination than face the attraction she was almost certain was mutual between them.

"Supplies should be here," he said, pointing to the drawer underneath the sink after following her. The bathroom would be considered large by anyone's standards but somehow shrank with the two of them inside alone.

Odette focused on clean teeth. Certainly, that would force her thoughts away from his broad chest and the fact he could be so tender with her despite his general size and physical conditioning.

Rafe stood at the door, resting his arms over his head against the doorjamb. Tension coiled inside her being this close to the handsome cowboy. A low fire started as sparks flew between their bodies.

His gaze appraised her, lingering on her lips after she blotted them with a hand towel. Turning, she nearly bumped into him. Odette put a hand up, her palm flat against a wall of a chest.

For a long moment, both stood there as though their feet were rooted. For reasons Odette didn't want to examine, she set her overthinking brain aside and went for what she wanted...a kiss.

The second her lips pressed against his full mouth, she realized how much trouble she was in with Rafe. The man was perfection and, in that moment, she'd done something uncharacteristic...she'd gone for what she wanted. Before the kiss could deepen, she pulled apart before risking any more. For another long moment, they both stood there, looking into each other's gaze. Connecting? Understanding? Searching?

She could feel his rapid heartbeat pounding underneath

her fingertips. It matched the tempo of hers. Stand here for much longer in the fog and haze that was Rafe, and she might do something else that was probably a bad idea. So, she cleared her throat to ease the sudden dryness and hoped that he could let this go. Her brain was already firing like a pinball machine on full tilt at all the reasons the kiss shouldn't have happened.

And then he brought his hand up to her chin, tilting her face for a better view.

"Don't beat yourself up, okay?"

∼

IT HAD BEEN one helluva day. Rafe realized exactly what was going on here. Odette was reaching for proof of life, proof the world was still good after a near-death experience. He'd read about these but never thought he'd be caught up in one. But he couldn't regret the kiss for reasons he didn't want to examine.

"I'm not. It's just that I'm not the kind of person who randomly kisses a near-stranger," she defended, casting her gaze down as she took a step back and folded her arms over her chest. The fact her cheeks turned six shades of red revealed her level of embarrassment. It was high, so he wanted to what he could to ease her heightened emotions.

"Never said you were," he said. "But I can't regret kissing you."

A deeper shade of red colored her cheeks. Hells bells, he hadn't meant to make the situation worse.

"All I'm trying to convey is that you've had a hard day and aren't thinking straight," he continued, searching for the right words. He'd never been much of a talker, but wanted to help Odette calm down for more reasons than the fact she carried his child.

Her grip tightened on her elbows as her body tensed. "I've had plenty of difficult days in the past. None led to me kissing someone without their permission."

"You had my permission," he corrected. "Bad idea or not, I was all in."

His comment made her crack a small smile and his chest filled with something that felt a lot like pride at being the one to put it there.

"That makes me feel a little better," she admitted. "Even though we both know it can't happen again."

"Agreed," he said. "And it won't."

A look of regret passed behind her eyes at the declaration. The words were probably coming out a little more enthusiastic because he was still trying to convince himself the kiss couldn't be repeated. Because when her lips had been pressed against his, he felt something stir in his chest that had been dormant far too long. Did Rafe want the kiss? Yes. Absolutely. No question. But it crossed a line.

This seemed like a good time to head back downstairs and grab a cup of coffee. Securing this place had been the easy part. Knowing what to do now that they were both here proved the real challenge.

Odette followed behind him as he moved into the kitchen. She took a seat at the granite island while he familiarized himself with the kitchen and threw a pod into the coffee machine. A few 'whirs' later, he had a fresh brew.

"Miracle," he said, holding up the mug. "Do you want a cup?"

"Can't," Odette said before he could rein the comment back in. Of course, she couldn't drink coffee. Not while she was pregnant. The caffeine wouldn't be good for the baby.

"Right. Sorry," he said, thinking she'd had to give up a whole lot more than just a morning cup. It had been easy to focus on his work at the ranch while she'd been out here, away from him. Her surprise about his family not knowing about the pregnancy had been niggling away at the back of his mind. Because there were other people who probably had a right to know about the baby now that everything was looking good and on track for a healthy delivery. "Do you want anything else? Water? Milk?"

"No, thanks," she said. "I'm good for now. Besides, I just brushed my teeth."

"Right," he said, leaning a hip against the bullnose edge of the countertop as he took another sip.

When he really thought about it, Odette might be a good sounding board. "Do you mind if I ask a question?"

She blinked a couple of times. "No. Not at all. Go ahead."

The fact she was nervous made him wonder what kind of question she believed he was going to ask.

"It's about Emile's family," he said, quashing any concern the question would have anything to do with the kiss. Their lips had barely touched. Could they even call what had happened a real kiss?

"Oh," she said. "Sure. I'll do my best to answer."

Rafe took a long, slow sip of coffee. The news about the baby was going to get out at some point. His brother Morgan was already on alert. The last thing he wanted to do was catch Emile's family off guard after all these years. But how did he begin to explain? "Emile was an only child."

"Ohhhhh," Odette said with compassion. She caught on to the implications without him needing to spell it out. "Are her parents alive?"

"Yes, ma'am," he informed.

"And you don't want them to hear this news through the grapevine," she continued.

"As unlikely as it is they would associate me having a child, with said child being their grandbaby, it doesn't seem fair not to clue them in," he stated. "It's been easy to keep all this under wraps considering the odds against it. Not to mention the fact doctors routinely recommend keeping a lid on pregnancy news through the first trimester."

Odette touched her belly. He wondered if she realized how many times a day she made the move.

"I've been pregnant for a while now," she said, glancing down before meeting his gaze. "We've been out of the woods for a long time despite the fact there are no guarantees. All the scans have been good. Sonograms have been coming back clear."

He'd opted out of knowing the sex of the child until it was born. Did she know? Should he ask?

"Losing Emile was like someone robbed my ability to breathe," he admitted for the first time. "I can only imagine what her parents must have been going through."

"You weren't close with her family?" she asked.

"No," he said. "Emile wasn't, either. They smothered her growing up so she had to keep them at arm's length for her own sanity."

"That could be a deep-down reason you've been holding back the information," she said. "In addition to the fact that you didn't want them to lose Emile twice."

Strange enough, that was exactly the reason he couldn't quite put into words. Rafe nodded. "On one hand, it seems selfish of me to keep this news to myself," he said. "After all, a pregnancy is good news. Right?"

"For some folks," she said. "Not everyone is excited about a baby."

"It's been five years since Emile died." Some days, it felt like she'd died an eternity ago. Others, it felt like yesterday. "Dredging up the past with her parents doesn't seem fair to them."

"Do you want this kid to know his or her grandparents on the mother's side?"

Rafe issued a sharp sigh. Truth be told, he wasn't so sure. He'd met Kaleb and Kylie Cassidy. They were the opposite of ranchers and, for a split second, he wondered if they would file for custody of the baby once the kid was born.

"Do you want to know something?" he asked, figuring that he might as well go all-in when it came to this conversation.

"Sure," she said.

"I don't think they would approve of using a surrogate after all this time." He took a sip of coffee to distract himself from the pull he felt at doing what most people would say was the right thing versus doing what Emile would have wanted. "Plus, Emile had cancer. Isn't there a possibility she could pass the gene along to the next generation?"

"I don't know," Odette said, rubbing her belly. "Genetics seem like a wildcard to me." She shifted in her seat. "I mean, don't get me wrong, there are certain conditions that are guaranteed to be passed down from one generation to the next. But cancer? They seem to be making progress against it all the time." She flashed her eyes at him. "I'm sorry it didn't work out for Emile. She sounds like a wonderful person who didn't deserve what happened."

He shook his head. "No. She didn't. She was all that was good in my world. If either of us had to go, it should have been me."

"Don't do that to yourself," Odette warned. "Survivor's guilt."

"Sounds like you have experience," he commented. The remark was off the cuff but hit the mark. Her eyes darkened, a solemn look overtook her features, and she nodded.

"My mother," she said. "I lost her almost a year ago."

Rafe came around the counter after setting down the mug. "Of course, I forgot. I'm sorry."

"Don't be," she countered. "It's not your fault."

"Still," he said.

"I was driving the car when we were hit by a vehicle that crossed over into our lane," Odette admitted. "I glanced down for two seconds when my phone holder came off the windshield." She paused a beat. "It should have been me and not her."

Rafe reached out to Odette, needing to be her comfort more than he needed air. She turned into him and burrowed into his chest as he looped his arms around her. Was this dangerous? Hell yes. But he couldn't fight his instincts.

# 7

Odette realized she'd gone down a slippery slope in talking about her mother's death. The conversation would, no doubt, only bring up more questions that she wasn't ready or willing to answer. This slip could make Rafe even more curious about her background, which wasn't something she could afford to have happen. It wouldn't take much to find her half-sister, and Odette couldn't allow it.

She sucked in a breath, pulled on her strength, and sat up, leaning against the back of the chair.

"I think you should have a conversation with Emile's parents," she said, figuring that was all it would take to throw water on the embers still simmering between them from earlier. Allowing Rafe to be her comfort was a mistake. One she didn't intend to repeat.

He stood there for a long moment like he needed a minute to shift gears. "Okay. Care to explain?"

"It's simple," she said a little stiffer than intended. "This involves their daughter. Wouldn't you want to know if you were in their shoes?"

"That's where it gets tricky," he said after a long pause. "I'm not sure I would. Not if the child wasn't going to play a significant role in my life."

"You don't want them involved?" she asked.

He walked around the granite island and retrieved his coffee mug. "I'd leave it up to them. They could be in the child's life. I guess." He placed the flat of his palm against the cool stone. "They weren't big fans of me being in Emile's life, and she kept them at arm's length for a reason."

"I understand all that, but wouldn't you want to know if you had a grandchild out there? Especially under the circumstances of losing your only child," she continued. It was none of her business and no one would blame Rafe for deciding to keep the baby a secret if the grandparents would be a bad influence. He was under no legal obligation to inform Emile's parents.

Rafe issued a sharp sigh. "Of course, I would."

"We could go tell them together," she offered, thinking it might be easier if they saw proof.

"I guess we could head out in the morning at first light."

"How far away do they live?" she asked.

"They're here in Austin over by the lake," he stated. "Fair warning, they might not be happy to see me. We haven't said one word since the funeral, where Emile's father made it known that I was only there by his good graces."

Odette wondered how long the squall had been brewing between the two men. "Did the two of you ever have words before then?"

He shook his head. "Not exactly. But Kaleb Cassidy works in banking. He wears a suit." Rafe held his hands up. "The man is more likely to have a manicure than a callous."

"So, he didn't think you were good enough for his

daughter?" She figured she already knew the answer to the question, but it never hurt to ask.

"That's an understatement." Rafe laughed. "Kaleb went to the University of Texas. He pledged a fraternity. He's the kind of guy who slaps you on the back and orders another round. He's loud and opinionated, and never wrong in his mind."

"Sounds like a jerk," she said.

"Not to his clients or the people he deems worthy of being in his presence," Rafe stated.

"He must have known you're a Firebrand," she said. "Didn't the name carry weight?"

"Some," he admitted. "In the beginning, at least. But the minute he found out I'd rather work cattle than sit behind a desk, he wrote me off."

"Families can be complicated," she agreed. More than Rafe knew. Hers would be classified as a hot mess by anyone in the know. Guy was the biggest jerk to Odette's mother. She still, for the life of her, didn't understand what her mother had seen in the man. Robin Mathers had had Odette when she was young. Caring for a baby caused Robin to drop out of her senior year of high school. Having a child had condemned her life to being an hourly worker since she didn't have enough money to put herself through school. There was no family support, either. The relatives Odette had, which weren't many, were barely scraping by. Her mother distanced herself, not wanting them to influence Odette. So, yeah, families could be all kinds of complicated.

"Kylie Cassidy was a different story," Rafe said. "She warmed up after she saw how much her daughter and I loved each other."

"Maybe we should tell her first, when she's alone," Odette said.

"I wouldn't want to put her in a bad position of having to hide something or feel like she had to lie to her husband," he said. "We could swing by tonight, rather than wait until tomorrow."

A glance at the clock said they'd been talking for longer than Odette realized. She bit back a yawn. Food was a priority. The little one inside her was growing, as was her appetite. "Is there anything for dinner in the fridge? Maybe we could go after we eat."

Rafe studied her for a long moment.

"How about this? We heat up something for dinner, have a sit-down meal, and then get ready for bed," he offered. "The talk I need to have with Emile's parents has waited this long. One more night won't hurt."

"Are you sure?" she asked. "I know how these things can be and, sometimes, it's best to get it over with once you work up the nerve."

He casually walked over to the fridge before opening the door. "My nerves are fine. Food is more important right now anyway. Can't have you or that little one going hungry."

"What do you have in there?" she asked, grateful for a break in the tension. The long day wore on her. The short nap did nothing to make a dent in how tired she was. And her emotions were all over the place. This seemed like a good time to remind herself that she'd kissed Rafe out of the blue if that said anything about her mental state. To be fair, he was easy on the eyes and caused her pulse to race just by being in the room.

Overwrought hormones?

Odette hoped so. Either way, she couldn't lose focus on why she was really here. The truck driving through the window of the restaurant earlier had been a stark reminder of dangers being present. If Guy found her, he would stop at nothing to get his daughter Andie back. The man wasn't just mean, he was evil. Once Odette finished her commitment to Rafe and handed over the baby, she had to grab her seven-year-old sister and run so they could start a new life with the funds.

In fact, now that she was in the final weeks of pregnancy, it might be a good time to reach out to the lawyer she'd researched to have her name legally changed. Times like these had her thinking about her mother, the beatings she refused to acknowledge, and the man she'd been afraid to leave.

"Pasta or ribs?" Rafe asked after clearing his throat.

Odette glanced up to find him staring at her. How long had that been going on? And why did one look from this man cause her pulse to kick up a few extra notches?

∽

"Pasta sounds good," Odette finally answered.

Rafe had no idea what was going on with the beauty sitting at the granite counter, but she'd been so deep in thought his food question had gone right over her head. He'd had to repeat himself to get her attention. Considering they were the only two people in the room, she must have gone somewhere else, far away in her head. There was a sad quality to her blue eyes that could be explained by the loss of her mother. For reasons he couldn't explain, though, he thought there was more to the story. She'd opened up to him, which he figured wasn't a common occurrence for her. Odette was the kind of person who held her cards close to her chest. So he liked the fact she felt comfortable enough around him to share something so personal.

After pulling the spaghetti and meatballs containers from the fridge and heating them, he pulled out a couple of plates and set the table.

"I can help if—"

"Your turn to be spoiled," he said, cutting her off. "No arguments."

Odette bit down on her bottom lip. Was she trying to stop herself from arguing? He figured as much, so he cracked a self-satisfied smile as he filled water glasses and brought them over to the dining table.

"This looks nice," she said as she joined him. He pulled her chair out for her. "I usually eat my meals in front of a screen, either TV or laptop."

He was guilty of doing the same. "It's easier to flip on a game or catch up on paperwork that way."

"Thank you for this." She sat down and then picked up a fork. "This smells amazing and looks even better, if that's even possible."

"I make no promises for the taste," he quipped. "This was all arranged by the Realtor who sold me this place."

"You *bought* this townhouse?" she asked.

"Figured it would be nice to have a place in Austin," he said. "This was Emile's hometown, so I wanted her child to have a connection to her." He'd opted not to find out the sex of the baby until the birth. Although, he could admit to a growing curiosity. Having Odette here and seeing her belly made it all feel so much more real.

"That's thoughtful," she said in between bites. A mewl of pleasure escaped as she chewed. "This is so good. We definitely need to order more of these dinners."

"You can have anything you want," he said, happy to see

a smile on her face after all the heavier conversation. "While you're here."

Rafe wasn't sure why he'd added those last three words. All he knew for certain was they'd slipped out as maybe more of a reminder to himself not to get too comfortable.

"Of course," she said with a little defensiveness in her tone. Rafe bit back a curse. He hadn't meant to say something to build more walls between them. One had come up the second he'd thrown that out there.

If she knew the sex of the baby, she might not be inclined to tell him now. What the hell? He wanted to know and she might have the answer.

"Do you know if you're carrying a boy or a girl?" he asked.

Odette stiffened like there was a sudden chill in the air. "No. Why would I? I'm a temporary home to this child, nothing more. There's no reason for me to know anything personal."

"So, you don't want to know? Not even on the day?" he asked, a little surprised at her answer. He understood on some level the need to keep a distance from the situation. But she'd been carrying this living being for months on end. Her body had morphed and, from everything he'd read on the topic, her hormones were completely out of whack.

"I already answered the question," she said before focusing all her attention on the plate in front of her.

The rest of the meal was spent in silence. A wall had come up alright. Rafe doubted he could break it down with a jackhammer at this point. Once plates were empty, Odette stood up and cleared the table. His moment of protest was met with a stiff arm.

He got it. He'd crossed a line. He was sorry.

But she was done.

Since he didn't want to frustrate her to the point she felt the need to leave the townhouse, he left well enough alone. He'd read a blog from another surrogate who'd documented the journey. The blogger had a difficult time separating from the baby once the job was done. Job? It wasn't like punching a clock at a bank. This could be a highly emotional journey according to the blogger.

Odette had the ability to shut down her feelings like no one he'd ever met before. It was like a wall came up in her eyes too, a blankness like there was a layer in between that dulled the spark.

Rafe bit back another curse. The two had been breaking down barriers all day. Finding himself right back where he started with her frustrated him. It was his fault. He'd asked the wrong question and, like a caged animal, she'd retreated to a corner. Keep pressing and she would lash out.

Rather than verbally apologize, he vowed not to bring the subject up again. Getting too close to Odette would be a mistake anyway. Where would it go? A surrogate was a means to an end, a business arrangement. He needed to keep those thoughts close at hand so he didn't make the same error in judgment. Once she delivered the baby, there was no reason for the two of them to continue a relationship. She would have performed her end of the agreement and would move on.

Besides, he hadn't considered the possibility that knowing him would create future pain. Was Odette attached to the child? Was there any chance she wouldn't be? She was human after all. She'd been caring for someone who had been growing inside her. There didn't need to be a genetic connection for Odette to feel attachment. He'd read something about it, but immediately went into business mode figuring she knew what she was getting into with the agreement. Did she? Was it possible to maintain emotional distance?

"Are you sure I should take the master?" Odette asked, breaking into his heavy thoughts.

"Go ahead," he urged.

She seemed uncomfortable with the idea.

"I doubt I'll get much sleep anyway," he said. "Besides, I tested out the guestroom bed and it'll work fine for the few hours of sleep I get every night. Go ahead and take the master. It has the most privacy anyway."

Odette stared at him for a long moment, looking like she was holding back. A few seconds later, she took a deep breath, put her chin to her chest, and then headed for the stairwell.

## 8

Odette slept in fits and starts. By the time the sun peeked through the slats of the miniblinds, she was wide awake and more than ready to get out of bed. She reached a hand behind her to put pressure on the spot on her back that ached the most as she waddled—not walked—to the bathroom.

Cramps were the norm now and the tightening in her abdomen was explained as Braxton Hicks contractions. They made her feel uneasy but not in pain now that she knew what they were. When they'd first started, she thought she was in the beginning stages of labor, which had freaked her right out.

After freshening up in the bathroom, she changed into a cotton maternity dress and sweater. The oversized cotton blend wasn't tagged as maternity wear but it might as well have been for how well it covered her bump. To be fair, she might *feel* huge, but she wasn't. Twenty-five pounds wasn't the end of the world. They were, however, concentrated around her midsection, putting an enormous amount of pressure on her lower back. And then, the kiddo seemed to be preparing for a black belt in karate most days. She'd joked to herself about nurturing a future soccer player, ballerina, or martial artist. Time would tell.

This seemed like a good time to remind herself that she wouldn't be along for the entire journey. She wouldn't know the sex of the child, let alone whether or not the kid grew up to play sports.

She heaved a sigh. This whole surrogate business was harder than she expected it to be. Sure, she'd read the books stating emotional attachment was a real risk. But Odette didn't think those warnings would apply to her. She'd always been able to handle herself and keep a distance from the world. She'd completely underestimated how personal a pregnancy would be. Then again, she had zero experience in this area. Kids weren't something she'd ever wanted to have. Besides, she was going to have her hands full with a certain seven-year-old.

Speaking of whom, Odette moved to the nightstand and grabbed the locket she always wore. It was taking a risk to keep her mother's prized possession around Odette's neck. But one she had to take. Inside the left-hand side of the locket was a picture of Odette as a baby and on the right was Andie. Odette couldn't afford for anyone to tie her to Andie while she continued to execute the plan, least of all Guy. Her muscles tensed at the thought of her former stepfather.

Odette absently fingered the delicate details of the locket, wishing like everything her mother was still here. A rogue tear escaped, rolling down her cheek, leaving a trail. She sniffed and tucked those emotions down deep. Let them out now and the deluge might never stop. Being pregnant made her soft. She would cry at a TV commercial if it pulled the right heartstrings.

Reminding herself to suck it up, she squared her shoulders and headed toward the top of the stairs. The smell of baked goods filled the hallway as she took the steps one at a time until she hit the landing on the first floor. The nice thing about being given the master was that it was located on the second floor instead of the third. One set of stairs was enough for her to bite off at a time. She realized she'd have to tackle another, if they were to leave today in order to visit Emile's parents.

Odette caught herself cradling her bump at the thought of the child growing up without a mother. Hers might have been a hot mess much of the time and definitely prone to getting involved with the wrong men, but Robin'd had a heart of gold and loved her daughters with everything inside her.

Was she misguided in relationships with men? The answer was a resounding *yes*. Was she perfect? The answer was a resounding *no*. Was she going to be missed every single day for the rest of Odette's life? *Absolutely.* The cavern in her chest would never be filled by anyone else. Rather than dwell on something she couldn't change, Odette poured her efforts into saving Andie.

It was probably too much to hope Guy would give up and walk away. Yesterday's 'accident' had rolled around in her thoughts most of the night. More questions flooded her with no easy answers, and she couldn't help but wonder if Guy had anything to do with the incident that could very well have cost her life. Her body involuntarily shivered at the thought Guy had caught up to her.

But why make it look like an accident? Why not just take her out? Or follow her?

The simple answer was that he would get off easy that way. If there was an accident that took her life, he wouldn't go to jail. And he wouldn't be able to locate his daughter—

nothing more than another possession to him—if he was behind bars.

Guy had never cared about Odette, which had been fine with her.

Smells from the kitchen interrupted her train of thought, offering a welcomed distraction.

"Hey," she said as she entered the space, not wanting to catch Rafe off guard. His back was turned to her as he pushed buttons on the microwave.

"You're up early," he said without a backward glance. Could she blame him after the way she'd snapped at him last night before leaving the room?

"Right," she said quietly.

"How did you sleep?" he asked, his voice sounding a little hopeful that she'd gotten good rest at least.

"Rough night," she admitted, not wanting to lie.

He had on a similar outfit as the previous night, a black t-shirt and jeans that hung low on his hips. He was barefoot on the tile flooring, which was another thing she probably didn't need to notice about the man.

"Was the bed responsible?" he asked.

"No," she said. "Nothing like that. Actually, it was comfortable. It's me. I tossed and turned." She placed her hand on her back and pushed her stomach out to ease some of the pressure on her spine. "Some days I think I'm carrying a bowling ball instead of a baby."

The microwave beeped, so he opened the door and pulled out a plate. "This is some kind of breakfast scramble, like a skillet breakfast, if you're interested."

"I can heat one for me," she said. "Go ahead and eat."

"It's already done," he argued with a look that said he was determined. He'd brought her to this place to 'take care' of her so she could sit back and do less. She had news for him. The deposit he'd paid for the business arrangement pretty much guaranteed she didn't have to do any heavy lifting. She hadn't worked at a real job since the first payment hit the bank.

Rather than argue, and lose, she walked over to the granite counter and grabbed a chair. This seemed a good place to sit for breakfast.

"Well, thank you," she said as he set a plate and fork down in front of her.

"You were drinking milk yesterday," he commented.

"That's right," she confirmed. It shouldn't warm her heart that he remembered, especially since it wasn't for personal reasons. He was probably just taking note because of the health of the baby.

He shot a look that basically asked if she'd like a glass now. She nodded before picking up the fork.

"How about you?" She turned the tables. "Did you sleep last night?"

His dark hair was still damp from a shower and a bead of water rolled down his neck, dropping onto his shirt. She shouldn't notice these things about him, so she refocused on the plate.

"I didn't," he said while fishing out another container from the fridge. "I don't need a whole lot and, besides, I wouldn't have been able to close my eyes for long." He worked magic with the microwave and joined her a few minutes later as she dug into her breakfast.

"Why not?"

"Facing Emile's folks," he began before stabbing a fork into a hunk of sausage.

"You don't strike me as the kind of person who would shy away from a challenge," she said after a thoughtful pause. "What are you afraid of?"

"The people?" he balked. "Nothing. The memories of being in that house with her...that's a whole different story."

Odette saw the haunted look in his eyes when she talked about his late girlfriend. It was no wonder five years had passed without anyone coming close because they were competing with a ghost. No one could measure up.

~

Rafe took a bite and chewed. He didn't talk about Emile with anyone but he guessed it was only fitting to think about her now. Five years had gone by without her. There was still a picture of her from when they were together beside his bed on the nightstand. Every morning, he woke to her smiling face and every night she was the last person he looked at before going to sleep.

Five years in a time warp, wishing a magic machine could take him back to the place when they were together, and he was happy.

Odette seemed content to leave the comment alone. She finished her plate in record time, indicating that she was hungrier than she let on. He needed to make a mental note of that, because he figured she didn't want to come across as demanding or a pain in the backside. She most likely wouldn't ask for something if she didn't really need it.

After dishes were put away, he walked over to the counter with his truck keys inside a basket. "I can make this a quick trip. There's plenty of food in the fridge and—"

"Hold on a second," she interrupted. "You aren't planning to go without me, are you?"

"I figured it might be neater this way," he said, searching for the right words.

"Because?"

When she asked the question, her forehead wrinkled in the darned cutest way. It wasn't something he wanted to notice about her. He didn't need to learn all the little quirks that made her unique. He'd crossed a line. One he didn't intend on violating again. Having her along for the ride might just make him become even more comfortable with her, and that would be another mistake.

"After last night, I figured you'd like to keep to yourself as much as possible," he said.

"Oh. Right," she said, sounding caught off guard. "Have I mentioned how much my moods have been swinging these past few weeks? I'm crying one minute and laughing the next, it seems."

Rafe couldn't say he related, but then his body wasn't undergoing the transformation hers was. "Does that mean you want to come with me?"

He wasn't certain it was a good idea, but that didn't stop him from asking.

"I would," she said. "It might be easier for the family to accept a pregnancy they actually see with their own eyes."

The closed-off quality to her eyes had temporarily receded. Could the two of them visit the folks who were supposed to be his in-laws?

"Okay," he said. "Throw on shoes and let's head out before Kaleb leaves for the office."

Odette's smile shouldn't warm his heart. He wouldn't exactly call her moods Jekyll and Hyde, but the swing was pretty hardcore.

Not three minutes later, they were sitting in his truck and the garage door was opening. The place was locked up tight, alarm set. To be honest, he didn't want to leave her alone in the townhouse, even for a few hours.

The real reason he'd stayed awake last night was to

analyze the events of yesterday. He'd checked the windows to make certain they were locked, something he never thought twice about at home, and had looked for any places the home might be vulnerable. Being paranoid was foreign to him, despite growing up on a ranch where chasing dangerous poachers off the property was a standard part of the job.

There was something off about the incident from yesterday afternoon that he couldn't quite put his finger on. Of course, his fear that this could be retaliation or revenge for his mother's actions wasn't something to be taken lightly.

Could there be something from Odette's past causing a threat? Since he didn't know much about her, he had to take the possibility into account. She'd lost her mother. Odette blamed herself. Was she hiding from someone? As much as he didn't want to pry into her personal life any more than necessary, assessing a potential threat could keep her alive.

Was he overthinking yesterday?

The only thing Rafe knew for certain was that he would never forgive himself if anything happened to Odette or the baby on his watch. Damn. Those words struck like a physical blow.

"What are you thinking about?" Odette broke through his heavy thoughts.

Rafe issued a sharp sigh. "How dangerous this world is."

"It can be," she agreed.

"And how I might be crazy bringing something so small and helpless into it," he continued, surprised at his own raw honesty. Rafe didn't normally do fear or regret. Both were like stalkers in a dark alley, closing in.

Odette reached across the console and touched his arm. Fissions of electricity sparked at the point of contact. He forced calm over his body. This wasn't high school and she wasn't a crush. He was a grown-ass man and she was the surrogate carrying his child. The only reason the two of them had any acquaintance at all was due to their business arrangement. The child she carried belonged to him and Emile. Period. There was no room for anyone else in the equation.

"We do the best we can," Odette said in a surprisingly calm and soft voice. She had the kind of voice that traveled all over him. "Bringing a child into the world means hope. Hope that things will improve. Hope that another brilliant mind can help fix some of the problems we face. Hope that people are still good in their purest form."

The revelation caught him completely off guard. The honesty and sense of hopefulness that came from the heart when she spoke.

Rafe took in a deep breath. "Maybe you're right. A baby is a fresh start."

"It'll be from scratch," she said, not moving her hand from his arm. The connection brought a sense of calm over him. She was all campfires and a blanket of velvet across a night sky. Thousands of stars twinkling down at him, winking, reminding him there were secrets hidden there most would never begin to understand.

"To be honest, I decided to take this chance to leave the outcome to fate," he admitted. "More than once, I haven't been certain I'm up to the task."

"I'm not a parent, so take this advice for what it's worth. But I have a feeling you will feel differently once you hold this little thing in your arms," she soothed. Her voice combined with those words almost had him believing it.

"Believe me when I say that I'm not fishing for compliments here," he said. "But what keeps me awake at night is the feeling I'm going to let Emile down by not raising this child right."

"You won't," she said without hesitation. How could she be so certain? "The reason I know is because your demeanor changes when you talk about this little bean. Your voice softens and becomes more protective. You would lay down your life to protect this growing bean and the two of you haven't even met yet."

Truer words had never been spoken.

"There's something primal about knowing there's a little one growing inside your belly, that brings out a different side of me," he admitted, realizing she was right on many levels. "It was easy to avoid thinking about the pregnancy most of the time because, for one, I didn't see you every day, and the second reason is that I'm still pinching myself that it's real."

"Believe me," she began as she rubbed her belly. "There's nothing fake about the legs on this kid."

Rafe smiled. He should probably be more freaked out about the baby's pending birth but being with Odette gave him a sense of calm like he'd never known before.

Stopped at a redlight, she tugged at his arm.

"Want to feel your child move?"

Rafe's heart clenched and he realized that he was in big trouble with this woman.

## 9

Odette couldn't ignore the connection between her and Rafe any more than she could deny her attraction to the man. However, there was a difference between having feelings and acting on them.

But when Rafe's hand extended over her belly, it was like a bomb detonated in the center of her chest. Her pulse kicked up a few notches, betraying her intention to remain calm at all costs.

Thankfully, he withdrew his hand after the baby kicked. Did he or she realize this was their father? His voice would be new. At this point, the little person had only heard Odette's. Would the little bean—correction, *baby*—confuse her as their mother?

The light changed, Rafe gripped the steering wheel, and Odette focused on the stretch of road in front of them. Traffic was heavy in Austin, even at this early hour. The sun was bright against the windshield. Odette blinked a few times, trying to get her bearings more than anything else. Being in the cab of a truck with Rafe's hand on her stomach shouldn't qualify as one of the most intimate moments of her life.

This reaction could be explained by the fact she missed her mother and her younger sister. Family was a foreign word to Odette now that her mother was gone. Part of the reason she'd been willing to be a surrogate had to do with the fact she never planned to be a biological mother. Raising her sister would be the most maternal thing she ever planned on doing.

Seeing her mother's mistakes with men and, honestly, making enough of her own, had Odette thinking marriage and family wasn't in the cards for her. Dating one person at a time, however, was and there were plenty of options for a single woman who didn't want to be in a serious relationship.

So, why was being near Rafe putting pictures in her head? Pictures of the two of them lazing around on a Sunday morning. Pictures of the two of them at various stages of the life they'd built together. Pictures of the two of them with the little...*baby.*

Odette gave herself a mental head slap as Rafe pulled into the driveway of a beautiful home on the hills of Lake Travis. He hopped out of the driver's side and came around to open her door, then offer a hand. Lightning struck the second their hands touched, causing her to suck in a breath. She did her best to cover, walking away before she gave away her traitorous body's reaction to him.

"I have no idea how the Cassidys will react to you," he warned. The croak in his throat provided a small sense of satisfaction that he was being just as affected by the chemistry between them.

"I'd be shocked if they weren't caught off guard considering I'll be standing next to you, pregnant," she said, clearing her throat.

"It's been five years since we've seen each other, so I have no idea if they want me to darken their doorway ever again," he stated as he caught up and then took the lead as though he needed to put a protective barrier between her and the door.

As Rafe reached for the front door, it opened. A young blond-haired, blue-eyed man filled the frame.

"Hey, Spencer," Rafe started as they stared into wide eyes.

"What are you doing here?" Spencer asked, his gaze bouncing from Odette's stomach to Rafe and back. Spencer sized her up, and a creepy-crawly feeling came over her at the perusal.

"Odette Barnes, meet Emile's cousin," Rafe continued, undeterred by the reaction.

"Nice to meet you, Spencer," Odette said, extending a hand.

The mid- to late-twenty-year-old stared at her hand like it was a bomb about to detonate. So much for a warm welcome. Odette retracted her hand and wiped down her cotton dress to clean off the sweat.

"What are you doing here, man?" Spencer asked. She could almost see the explosions happening inside his skull.

"I'm here to see Kaleb and Kylie," Rafe continued. "I need to speak to them both and I thought it would be best to drop by before Kaleb headed into the office.

Spencer stepped outside and closed the door behind him. His appraisal of Rafe had the man standing a little straighter and balling his fists at his sides like he was preparing for a fight. Spencer was half a foot shorter than Rafe and not nearly as buff. A fight wouldn't last a minute, and Spencer seemed to know it. He put his hands up in the surrender position, palms out, as he took a step back.

"You sure this is a good idea?" Spencer asked. The guy had on a button-down shirt with metal buttons. "It's been a long time and I don't think they would appreciate the blast from the past."

Rafe fished his cell out of the front pocket of his jeans and then held it up. "I still have both of their numbers in my contacts. A quick call can make you move." Then he shot Spencer a look that would have frozen water on an August sidewalk in Texas. "Or I could just move you." He paused a beat. "Your choice."

Odette was pretty certain Spencer started shaking after the threat. He immediately reached for the door handle behind him but the door swung open mid-reach. A large, intimidating figure filled the doorframe. This had to be Kaleb Cassidy.

"What the hell are you doing here?" the older man asked. His size was intimidating to Odette but Rafe didn't flinch. To be fair, he had an inch of height and a whole lot more muscle.

"I came to see you and Kylie."

"The party planner isn't due for another hour," came a singsong voice from behind the large frame blocking a visual into the home.

Rafe folded his arms over his chest and shot a look that dared Kaleb or Spencer to make a move.

"We have a visitor, honey," Kaleb said, stepping inside the home and dragging Spencer along with him.

"Who is it?" The middle-aged woman was well put together, even this early in the morning. She had short auburn hair that was fashionably styled. She had on a designer velvet sweatsuit that highlighted a body that was still in good shape. Manicured nails came with just the right amount of makeup to bring out the vibrancy of her brown eyes and olive features.

"Rafe Firebrand," she exclaimed. "Is it really you?" Her surprise quickly morphed into a smile. Kylie might be warm, but her husband stood there, coldly staring at Odette's bump. Instinctively, she cradled the baby as Rafe stepped in front of her. Was he putting himself physically between her and a threat?

As much as Odette didn't like Kaleb, she didn't trust Spencer. Keeping one eye on him, she followed Rafe inside the home.

White marble floors led to a wall of windows in an open if not cold, modern space. The view to the lake was incredible and softened the hard lines of the furniture and décor.

"Coffee?" Kylie asked after introductions were made. Unlike her husband, she barely glanced at the bump. In fact, it almost looked like she was actively avoiding the stomach area.

"No, thank you," Rafe said as the group of five made their way into the kitchen.

Spencer trailed behind them. Out of the corner of Odette's eye, she caught Kaleb and Spencer exchanging glances. The men clearly didn't want Rafe—or her for that matter!—anywhere near this home.

Their reaction was understandable on some level, and yet she had the overwhelming urge to keep them in her sights at all times.

~

"Thanks for seeing me," Rafe said to Kylie. His one-time future mother-in-law had warmed up to him once she'd realized how in love Rafe and Emile had been. At some point, she must have realized there was no use in fighting against it and surrendered to love as much as they had.

"You're welcome here anytime," Kylie said after giving a scowl to her husband and nephew. "I hope you won't be a stranger."

Her warm reception helped pave the way for what he needed to say.

"Please, sit down," Kylie said, motioning toward the bar chairs stacked around the oversized white marble island. Everything about this home was over-the-top and in good taste. It wasn't his taste in particular, but he figured more than one decorating magazine would have a field day highlighting the Cassidy home in their pages. Emile's taste had leaned towards her mother's, whereas Rafe was more of a worn leather chair and metal star above a tumbled stone fireplace kind of guy.

"I'm good with standing," Rafe said after deferring to Odette. She'd refused with a slight head shake.

"What brings you here after all this time?" Kylie asked, still ignoring the elephant in the room. The woman did, however, glance at Rafe's ring finger.

"I have news and I'm not sure how to go about telling you," he hedged.

"You've met someone," Kylie said with a slightly shaky voice.

"Actually, no," he said, figuring he better just get on with it. Words weren't exactly his specialty, so he was likely to mess this up anyway. Might as well go for broke. "My friend Odette is carrying my child, though."

Kylie's eyebrows drew together. "I'm afraid I don't understand unless this is some type of modern arrangement. Why come here?"

"Because this directly involves you and your husband," he continued. "Odette is a surrogate and she's carrying mine and Emile's baby."

Kylie's jaw nearly dropped to the marble flooring. A grunt issued from Kaleb that sounded more animal than human, and Spencer's eerie quiet had the hairs on the back of Rafe's neck standing up. Emile had been concerned about her younger cousin after he'd moved in to the family home six years ago. Even more, she'd been worried about her mother, since Spencer seemed to have been thrown out of prep school. Kaleb had volunteered to help his nephew out of trouble with the law and, as it looked, the two had formed a bond that made them thick as thieves in the years since. Her mother had confided in Emile that she didn't trust having Spencer in the house. From the looks of it, the situation worked out all right.

"What? How? When?" Kylie's mouth finally formed words as she brought a hand up to her forehead. Horror battled with shock across her features.

"After Emile's diagnosis, she surprised me by having her eggs retrieved before she started treatment," he explained. "I never intended to do anything with them, but she wanted to have a family once she beat..."

He had to stop for a few seconds to pull himself together. Talking about Emile and her plans was taking more of a toll than he expected. So much for pulling off a tough-guy routine. Then again, he'd always been soft when it came to matters of the heart, which was another reason he'd closed his off after Emile. Weakness wasn't exactly something he leaned into.

"Are you telling me that 'thing' inside her belongs to my baby girl?" Kaleb piped in with the kind of anger in his voice that almost made the floor shake.

Rafe bucked up for a fight.

"The 'thing' you're referring to happens to be mine and Emile's child," Rafe said through clenched teeth. "And your grandchild."

A sob escaped from Kylie. "My baby's baby?" She made a beeline for Odette, eyes locked onto the round belly. "I'm going to have a grandchild?" She stopped when she was almost toe-to-toe with Odette, who reached out for Rafe's arm. The move caused Kaleb's eyebrow to shoot up and an angry sneer to form on the man's lips.

"Everything is healthy so far and the baby is due in four weeks, give or take," Rafe informed Kylie.

She dropped down to her knees in front of a mortified Odette, who took a step back. He should have predicted this meeting would have ended up being emotional. To be honest, he'd thought the family would kick the two of them out before it got this far. But here they were. Seeing him again would have been enough to dredge up old hurt. Losing a child, no matter the age, went against the natural order of life. Rafe couldn't imagine a worse pain.

"I'm sorry," Kylie said as tears streamed down her face.

A frustrated Kaleb huffed as he walked over to his wife and practically jerked her to her feet by her elbows. "Stand up and quit embarrassing yourself." He glared at Rafe, who'd taken a step forward. Were it not for a look from Kylie, Rafe might have done something stupid. Like throw a punch.

Then again, he didn't need to end up in jail when Odette needed him most.

"There's no need to apologize," Odette reassured. She'd tensed up the minute Kaleb walked over to his wife. Her hands fisted, causing him to realize she had the same thought of throwing a punch. The momentary flinch before she regained control told him there'd been some type of abuse in her background.

Could he ask her about it? Would she be honest? And, again, was she hiding from someone?

"I should probably sit down," Kylie said as she took a step back and placed a hand on the marble to hold herself upright.

"Please," he began. "Do what makes you comfortable."

"I'm going to sit down." Kylie kept a hand on the marble as she rounded the bullnose edge and then perched on a bar-height chair. "Join me?"

Odette followed suit, taking the spot one over from Kylie. Keeping distance was probably a good thing, so Kylie didn't reach out and touch the bump. Odette had proven brave in coming here. She must have known this would be emotional for everyone involved. While Kylie seemed to be all over the map on emotions, Kaleb had just the one...anger.

Rafe shouldn't be surprised. It had been the man's go-to emotion the entire time Rafe had known him. Emile had said her father's temper made her feel like she constantly walked on eggshells growing up in his house.

"What do you want from us?" Kaleb asked, bitterness lacing his words. "Money? Support?"

Rafe stared the man down, almost daring him to say another word. Then came, "I damn well don't want anything from you." He had to stop long enough to stem the flood of anger that rushed through his veins. "I thought you had a right to know about the baby. I've done my part now." He caught Odette's gaze. "Ready to go?"

## 10

Odette took a few seconds to consider her options. If they walked out the door now, would Rafe ever return? Kaleb was awful by anyone's standards. There was something off about Spencer that she couldn't quite pinpoint. But Kylie was all heart. She deserved to know her grandchild—a grandchild she clearly wanted to know.

"Would it be possible to sit here for another minute?" Odette asked, rubbing the bottom of her bump and taking in a breath. Stress wasn't good for her or the pregnancy, and this encounter was more than she'd bargained for.

"I'm not standing around here for another second," Kaleb fumed. "Spence, come on."

Before anyone could say another word, the pair stormed out the front door.

"He'll come around," Kylie reassured. "The pain of losing Emile is still fresh, even after all these years. It's like a wound that never gets better, never heals, and we have no idea how to make it better or ease it." Her shoulders sagged.

"I guess there's a feeling that if we get over her and move one, she somehow dies all over again."

Odette scooted over a chair. She had no idea what to say in a situation like this. She'd never experienced anything like it before and couldn't imagine the pain. The closest she'd come was losing her mother, and that was the worst kind of awful. She made eye contact with Kylie. "Do you want to feel the baby move?"

As much as Odette was uncomfortable being touched by a stranger, it seemed the best way to remind Kylie that her daughter had left a beautiful gift behind.

"I would like that very much," Kylie said as more silent tears streamed down her cheeks.

Odette took in a breath, "Go ahead. The baby just moved."

"I saw through your dress," Kylie said as she placed the flat of her palm on the spot. The little bean responded with a swift kick. Kylie's face lit up. "I just felt..." She looked to Odette and then to Rafe. "Her or him?"

Rafe shrugged. "No one knows." He went on to explain how slim the odds of this pregnancy coming to fruition had been, and that he'd left it to chance.

"It sounds like a miracle," Kylie said after a thoughtful pause. There was something oddly reassuring about the woman's touch. A mother's touch? Moments like this one had Odette missing her own mother something fierce.

Kylie withdrew her hand and then placed it on her lap. "Thank you for coming here today, Rafe. That couldn't have been easy for you."

"I owe some of the decision to Odette," he deflected. "She talked me into what I knew was a good idea."

"I'm glad she did," Kylie confirmed. "And don't worry about the boys. They'll figure out this is a second chance to be with our daughter." She scrunched up her nose. "That didn't sound right. Obviously, the baby isn't Emile. But it's from her." Kylie shifted her gaze to Odette. "She was our only child and our pride and joy."

"Emile sounds like an amazing person," Odette said, trying to squelch the emotion knotting in her throat. She shouldn't be jealous of a ghost. And yet, there it was. Carrying someone's child was clearly a tricky situation and was part of the reason Odette didn't want to live with Rafe. They'd had online, on-camera meetings. She knew what he looked like even though nothing prepared her for the full effect of standing in the same room. His physical presence ate up the space.

"Thank you for saying that," Kylie said. "Of course, it's easy to remember all the good once someone is gone."

Odette risked a glance at Rafe, who gave a slight nod of agreement.

"I guess we all look back with rose-colored glasses," Kylie continued. "The truth is easy to shove aside, even though Emile had basically cut off contact with her father and I before she met you." Kylie toyed with the zipper on her sweatshirt. "Were you the reason she called me up that spring morning, to meet for coffee?"

Rafe gave another almost imperceptible nod. Odette got the impression he didn't want to take credit for the meetup.

"I knew it," Kylie said, slapping her knee. "I never asked but I always suspected."

"She loved you," he pointed out. "Her relationship with Kaleb was different. Once I pointed out that you shouldn't be punished for your husband's actions, she saw the light. So, it was Emile who decided to make the call. I just happened to be in the room to help her talk it out."

Kylie gave a resigned look. "I should have been a better mother."

"Your daughter loved you."

"That might be true," Kylie said. "But did she respect me? Did I give her a reason to look up to me?"

"Only Emile would be able to answer those questions," Rafe said. "And it's never too late to change."

Kylie studied Rafe for a long moment. Then, she got up and walked over to an iPad. She tapped on the screen a few times and music filled the space. She walked to the front door and then presumably checked to see if the men were gone. What was going on with the paranoia?

"I'm leaving him," Kylie whispered after reclaiming her seat. She perched on the edge and leaned toward them both as Rafe moved beside Odette. "It's been in the works for months now. I have a lawyer who is ready to go as soon as I make the call. I've been sneaking money into an account, which hasn't been easy when I live with a banker."

"What's the saying?" he asked. "Isn't it the cobbler's son who has no shoes?"

"Not in my house," Kylie confided. "It's the reason I didn't leave him a long time ago after losing my daughter while she was still alive. He controls the finances." Kylie hiccupped. "I lost her twice." She looked at Rafe with the most adoration and respect. "You brought her back to me twice."

"If money's an issue—"

"No, I couldn't take from you," Kylie cut him off. "Thank you for the offer. But I've been squirreling money away for years without Kaleb's knowledge. I get an allowance but shopped in second-hand stores for clothes instead of going to the places he thought I was. I came home with a designer sweater and he had no idea where it came from. I started early in our marriage on my own mother's advice, rest her soul."

"Sounds like a smart woman," Rafe commented. Odette couldn't help but wonder how her own mother's life might have turned out if she'd done the same.

"She grew up in a time when a woman couldn't have a credit card in her name," Kylie said. "She made certain her only daughter knew a few tricks, in case I was left to my own devices."

"Do you need a place to stay?" he asked. "Because the ranch is always open to you."

"I promised myself that I wouldn't involve you or Emile," Kylie said. "There was no reason to involve either of you."

"Emile would have wanted to know," he said. "She would have helped."

"I couldn't put her in that position with her father," Kylie said. "Their relationship has been strained enough. I didn't want to contribute."

Odette bit back the urge to tell Kylie no one would have blamed her. She wondered if that was part of the reason her mother never spoke ill of Guy to Andie. When she really thought about it, kids were made up of both parents. Bad-mouthing one, forcing kids to take sides wasn't the best parenting. She had to give it to Kylie. The woman had endured a difficult marriage but held herself together well.

"Once Emile died," Kylie continued, "I didn't want to live either. I shut down. Believe it or not, my husband came to my side and told me to take all the time that I needed." She shook her head. "Funny how those moments stick in your mind. The few times they're nice to you. You cling to those moments and try to build a life from them. But the bad times…" Her body involuntarily shivered.

"Has he touched you?" Rafe's voice shook with anger.

"Water under the bridge now," Kylie said. Her gaze landed on Rafe's hands, that were fisted at his sides, and smiled sadly. Gently.

He took in a long slow breath. His shoulders relaxed a little as he flexed and released his fingers, no doubt to work out some of the tension.

"I'm not a violent man," he said, "especially with someone weaker than me. But when I hear about someone abusing their size or physical advantage…"

He didn't complete the sentence. Didn't need to. The understanding was clear.

Looking back, guilt washed over Odette. Why hadn't she spoken to her mother about Guy's abusive behavior? Would it have made a difference? What about the others before him? Would her mother have broken the cycle if Odette had raised a red flag instead of sitting quietly, thinking it wasn't her place to speak up?

Right then and there, Odette made a pact to speak her mind if she encountered abuse. And she planned to start right now.

## 11

"When do you plan to leave him?"

Odette's question seemed to catch Kylie off guard. "Soon."

"Don't wait," Odette pressed, surprising Rafe with the conviction in her tone. More evidence she was hiding from someone?

Kylie took in a long, slow breath. "You're right. I've waited long enough. I need to pull the trigger with my lawyer."

"Do you have a place to stay?" Rafe asked. He had no plans to walk out the front door until he knew she was going to be safe.

"Yes," she said. "But I can't tell you where." Kylie's gaze dropped to Odette's belly. "When did you say the baby was due?"

"In four weeks," he confirmed.

"I have your number," Kylie said. "Mine won't work after today."

Good. She was going to take action. Part of Rafe wanted to stick around to make certain she was able to break away without any conflict. But she would insist that he left and he shouldn't know where she was going because it could compromise her location.

"I'll expect to hear from you soon," Rafe said.

"When you get an unfamiliar number, pick up," she stated before giving him a big hug. She turned to Odette. "Can I hug you too? In a weird way, I feel connected to you."

"Of course," Odette said, standing up and embracing Kylie. It did Rafe's heart good to see these two women getting along for reasons he wasn't certain he wanted to spend a whole lot of time examining.

"Be careful," he warned. "And be safe."

"I will," Kylie promised. "Now you two get out of here. I have a grandbaby on the way and I want to be prepared."

Rafe ushered Odette into the truck. The morning had been productive and he wondered what else they could get done. "Do you want to swing by your place to pick up a few things? Clothes? Personal items?"

Odette didn't immediately answer and he could sense her hesitation. Was she afraid?

"We could swing by on the way home," he continued. "I'd be right there."

"It's not what you think," she countered, recognition dawning.

He wanted to hear her take on his thoughts. "What is that?"

"There's no one at home waiting for me," she said.

"What makes you think I believe that?" he asked, glad the subject had come up.

"You think I'm afraid to go home because someone is there or might be there, a boyfriend," she said flat out. He couldn't argue her point, so he didn't.

"There were things said inside the house that gave me

the impression you might be hiding out from someone," he said, tackling the sensitive subject as best he could.

"I can see why you would think that," she said after a thoughtful pause.

He started the truck's engine and navigated onto the main road leading out of the subdivision.

"My mom was in an abusive relationship," she said. "Not just one, actually. She seemed to be a magnet for men who liked to hurt women, whether it be physical or emotional. I think she mainly like overly possessive men. Maybe she saw it as a sign they loved her."

"Guys like that don't deserve relationships," he said, gripping the steering wheel a little tighter.

"No, they don't," she agreed. "And yet, they seem to find people who have maybe had a hard time in life or need the self-esteem push. The opposite ends up happening. At least, that was the case with my mother."

"I'm sorry," he said and meant it.

"So am I," she said. "Looking back, the worst part for me is that I never said anything to her about it. Now, I can't help but wonder if she thought I didn't believe she deserved better."

"I'm certain that's not the case," he said.

"How can you be so confident?" she asked, sounding genuinely confused.

"Because you cared about her, and still do," he said. "Because you talk about her with so much respect in your words and voice and that had to come through when you were with her too. And because you aren't the kind of person who would look down on her even when she made the wrong choices."

Odette sat there for a long moment that stretched on for half the ride home. "You were right about something." She glanced over at him. "A few things, actually, but one in particular. I'm afraid of her husband."

"Did he ever—"

"No, not me," she interrupted. "My mom didn't talk about it, but there were signs. Sunglasses on cloudy days. Too much eye makeup that seemed to be covering up something. The way she got extra nervous when he came home in a bad mood."

"You would have said something if you thought it might have made a difference," he reassured.

"What if it would have?" she asked.

"Life is full of uncertainty," he said. "Emile and I weren't on good terms when she got the diagnosis. I was out chasing poachers and my cell phone was off the grid. She had to spend three days with that news and no one to talk to about it. My last words to her before that awful day was that I needed time alone to figure out if I wanted a future. How much of a jerk was I?"

"We all make mistakes," she said, coming to his defense.

"Which is so easy to see in someone else and so hard to forgive in ourselves," he stated.

From the corner of his eye, he saw her nodding.

"It's so true," she agreed.

"Would your mother's husband come for you?" he asked. It would explain why she'd taken the surrogate job. A large lump sum of cash, enough to disappear, would definitely be attractive to someone who felt threatened.

"That's a good question," she said without conviction. She was hiding something and he intended to figure it out before she ended up hurt or worse.

"I can check into—"

"No," she said, cutting him off. "That won't be necessary.

Besides, once the baby is born, I plan to move far away from Texas."

"You have a thing against wide open skies and the color blue?" he asked, trying to lighten the mood before she closed up on him again.

"Nope," she said. "But change is good, right? It never hurts to start a new life somewhere else, somewhere you don't have any history."

Sounded like someone who wanted to run away to him. Pointing it out didn't seem like a good idea, so he stuffed the comment down deep and moved on.

"We may as well stop by my apartment, since I'm going to be at the townhouse for a few weeks," she conceded. "It'll be nice to have a few of my own things."

Before he could respond, she added, "Plus, I won't be moving back there once I hand over the package."

She'd called the baby 'little bean' earlier. He wondered if that was the term she used when she felt close to the child. Calling him or her 'the package' came across as cold and detached. Not that he could blame her. She was helping him in a huge way, and he had no idea how she was pulling it off without getting emotionally attached.

Getting attached to the surrogate, not to mention a woman who was determined to walk out of his life forever, would be the worst of a bad idea. So, he got it. And yet, his heart still argued otherwise. The connection he felt with Odette wasn't expected, wanted, or possibly even returned.

Tell the news to his heart.

∼

ODETTE HAD TALKED TOO MUCH. Period. Being around Rafe

even for a short time shifted her focus away from where it needed to stay...Andie.

She rattled off her address in Galveston. At nine o'clock in the morning, the seven-hour drive would put them in at four p.m., give or take if they drove straight through without stopping for food, gas, or lunch.

Since she'd tossed and turned all night, she laid the seat back and dozed off.

Three hours later, she blinked open blurry eyes and stretched out her arms. The truck was stopped and the driver's seat empty. Sitting up, she realized they were at a gas station. Not *a* gas station. *The* gas station. Buc-ees. The quintessential one-stop for literally everything a person could possibly want on the road, plus clean bathrooms and friendly workers.

The thought of food made her stomach growl, so she grabbed her handbag and exited the truck.

"Hey," Rafe's voice had a way of gliding through and around her, making her want things she couldn't have...*him*. "Hold up and I'll go inside with you."

"Can't wait," she said, needing to keep a little distance between them as much as possible. "Bladder."

The click from the gas pump indicated the tank was full. She picked up the pace. Once inside, the bathroom lived up to the reputation. The stalls were good, the lighting decent, and everything was hygienic. Spit-shine clean. She would never underestimate the power of a good bathroom on a road trip after the last fast food burger debacle. Don't even get her started because there was only so long a person could hold their nose. At some point during the transaction, she'd had to breathe. As it turned out, holding her breath made her take in a lungful of someone else's bad lunch decision.

Odette washed up and walked into the massive food and retail center. The smell of barbecue caught her attention, so she followed the scent to a made-to-order brisket sandwich station. After tapping the screen to put in her order, she wandered over to the refrigeration section and located a decaf tea, cold. She missed the boost of real caffeine, but this would do.

By the time she located a piece of fruit and wandered back to the brisket station, the sandwich was up.

The other great thing about this place? There were so many cashiers there was never a wait. Buc-ees had figured out how to keep people happy on the road and she appreciated them for it.

Sitting in the truck, she polished off the sandwich before Rafe returned. It occurred to her that she probably should have asked him if he wanted anything. She wasn't used to looking out for anyone else. It had just been her for so long. Now that she was responsible for Andie, that would have to change. Her half-sister was safely tucked away at a boarding school under a different name, thanks to the healthy deposit that Rafe had paid her.

Rafe was carrying a to-go box as he reclaimed the driver's seat. "Are you good on food?"

"I picked up a brisket sandwich," she said.

"There's a double stack of baby back ribs in here if you want some," he offered.

"Seriously?" she asked. "How did I miss those?"

"You didn't," he said with a smile before setting down the box on the console. He pulled into a parking spot and set up a makeshift picnic over the console.

The ribs were heaven. The fries even better.

"I didn't think to grab a drink for you," she said.

"I have water in the back." He reached around and grabbed a pair of bottles, handing one over.

When the meal was finished, he threw away the trash before navigating onto the highway.

"Did you get a little sleep?" he asked.

"Three hours of solid rest," she confirmed. "So much so that I was afraid I'd drooled all over my sweater."

Rafe laughed. "There wasn't enough to put out a fire."

It was Odette's turn to laugh. "Great."

"You also have the cutest snore," he continued, as if hearing that she'd dripped saliva down her chin wasn't enough embarrassment.

"Well, isn't that the best news," she teased. Did he just call her cute?

Before she went down the rabbit hole of reasons to be more attracted to Rafe, she changed the subject. "What did you think about the visit this morning?"

Rafe paused for a moment as though mentally shifting gears. His expression grew serious. "I hope Kylie follows through with leaving Kaleb."

"She will," Odette reassured. "There was a spark in her eyes that a woman gets once she's come to a decision."

"Good," he said. "Because she needs to get out."

"What about Spencer?" she asked. "The young man rubs me the wrong way."

"You caught the look exchanged between him and Kaleb," Rafe said. "I saw you out of the corner of my eye."

"It's like they were up to something," she agreed.

"Or were about to be," he stated.

"Do you think it's weird that he seemed to step right into Emile's footsteps?" she asked. "There were photos of him and her parents almost everywhere, and so few of her."

"She did stop talking to her parents for years after graduating high school," he pointed out. "Knowing her father, he ordered Kylie to remove any evidence she was their daughter."

"A man with a temper isn't a good person to be around," she said. "And that would explain the lack of family photos with Emile in them."

"The family wasn't on good terms until we started dating and even then, Emile became close with her mother again and not her father," he said. "I'm certain he blamed me for his daughter cutting him off."

"Didn't that happen before the two of you met?" she asked.

He nodded. "The timeline didn't seem to click with Kaleb."

"People see and believe what they want," she said. "The truth rarely comes into play with someone who is determined to block out evidence that disproves their theory once they lock onto an idea."

"The man knows how to dig his heels in," Rafe agreed.

"It's never wise to underestimate an abuser," she continued. "They know how to manipulate people's emotions. It's the reason people stay in abusive relationships."

## 12

Rafe had questions. Odette had opened up about her mother's situation, and he couldn't help but wonder if Odette had someone lurking in the background. There was something she wasn't telling him. He could sense it and his gut instincts about people were rarely wrong. This was bone-deep. He also knew when not to push a subject. Didn't mean he always followed his gut on that one but getting better about it was the goal.

The rest of the drive to Odette's apartment in Galveston was filled with easy conversation. Topics bounced around from how she'd been feeling each month of the pregnancy to the weather. At four-forty-five, they arrived in front of her small apartment complex building.

"Fair warning, this place isn't much," she said.

"It's just you, right?" he asked, but it was more statement than question.

"Yes," she agreed in a tone that said there was more to the story. Rafe wanted to know more about her. He wanted to know everything, but firing a bunch of questions at her would have the opposite effect; she'd bolt faster than a thoroughbred on race day. He had four weeks, give or take, depending on how things went with the pregnancy, in order to get to know her better.

Rafe parked and then rounded the front of the truck to open her door for her. After helping her climb down, she shouldered her handbag and then reached inside for keys.

The apartment complex was a two-story building with five apartments on each floor. The parking lot was small. There were a few spots for visitors. Mailboxes sat in the center island and another set of apartments was on the opposite side of the parking lot. It was like looking at a mirror.

Odette's place was the end unit, first story. He took note of the fact someone could easily get inside through a window of the brick building. There was no way a person could climb up the side of the brick building and the metal staircase caused enough noise to bring attention to any visitors.

He followed her to the door of apartment one. The odd numbers were on the bottom, even on top. The place was a studio, so it was easy to see the whole apartment once he stepped inside except for the bathroom. A simple bed was shoved up against one wall on the opposite side of the room. Next to it was a sofa and coffee table with an adjacent flat-screen TV.

The room was messy, which surprised him given how neat she'd been at the townhouse.

Odette stood two steps inside the door and glanced around. She muttered a curse.

"What is it?" he asked.

"Nothing," she said, dismissing his concern.

He didn't buy it. Especially when she made a beeline to

the counter and started opening drawers. More swearing told him she was in panic mode.

"What's wrong?" he asked, coming at the same question from a different angle.

She stopped long enough to tuck loose tendrils of hair behind her ears. After an exhale came, "Someone has been in here."

"What would they be looking for?" he asked. Jealous boyfriend?

Odette turned around and flashed apologetic eyes at him. "I'd rather not say."

Rafe issued a sharp sigh. "Normally, I would agree with you and drop the subject, but you're stressed, which isn't good for you or the baby, and I keep wondering if there's something I can do to help."

"This is personal and doesn't involve you," she quickly defended. Her response was almost robotic, like she'd been planning to say something like this for a while. Or at the very least had thought it through. It sounded too rehearsed to be off the cuff, and that was cause for even more concern.

Rather than put up an argument, he just stood there and stared at her.

"Fine," she conceded. "My life is intertwined with yours right now." She cradled her bump again. "I thought I was being way off base yesterday when I feared my mother's husband had something to do with the restaurant incident. But now, I'm wondering if Guy was behind it."

"Why would he come after you?" Rafe asked. "It wasn't your fault that your mother died."

Before the conversation could go any further, Odette froze.

"What?" he asked, following her gaze to the window in back of the property.

"Someone is here," she said. "I saw a dark figure lurking out there."

Rafe didn't have a weapon because he only carried when he was on the land in case he ran across a coyote. His Colt 45 was easier to have on hand.

Glancing around, he moved to the kitchen. "Where are your knives?"

"The drawer next to the oven," she said with panic in her voice.

Rafe cut across the room stealth-like and opened the drawer. He picked out a carving knife that looked half machete. "Lock yourself in the bathroom."

Odette shook her head. "Absolutely not. I'm coming with you."

He knew better than to argue when she got a certain look, a determined look. It was the look she had now. Since there was no time to explain why he would prefer she stay behind a locked door than follow him, he conceded with a nod.

"Where's the key?" he asked, holding out his free hand, palm up. A second later, it was being placed in his palm. He closed his fingers around it, ignoring the all-too-familiar frissons of heat pulsing from where their skin made contact.

Tucking her behind him, he moved out the front door into the bright sunshine. Metal glinted in the sunlight. He glanced around at the vehicles dotting the parking lot before bending down to pick it up and examine it. For better or worse, there was no change on the lot. The weirdly-shaped metal button came from one of those designer shirts. This belonged to Spencer.

Rafe stood before pocketing the item and locking the door, figuring it would be stupid to take a chance. Besides, a person might be trying to draw them out of the home so they could sneak inside and wait for the right moment to attack. Right bicep against the building, Odette tucked behind him, he made his way around the side of the building. Brushing against the brick with his arm, he slowly rounded the backside.

No one was there.

Had she imagined it? Was there a tree branch that she'd mistaken for a person? Or had the mystery guest rounded the other side before they made it outside?

"Which way did the figure move?" he asked.

Odette pointed to the opposite end. It made sense. He didn't like it.

Trees in the back might have caused the shadow, especially since wind gusted, despite the sunny temperature. His mind snapped to a few possibilities of who might have followed them here, not the least of which was Kaleb, Spencer, or both.

In fact, once they got back inside the apartment, Rafe fished out his cell phone and made a call to Kaleb's office.

The receptionist picked up on the second ring.

"Is Kaleb Cassidy in the office this morning?" he asked.

"Yes, sir," the perky voice confirmed. "May I ask who is calling?"

Rafe ended the call. It didn't rule out Spencer, but Kaleb had gone in to work. Rafe walked over to the bar-height counter separating the living and kitchen space. Mail was spread out. His gaze stopped at a maintenance ticket.

"Someone came in and sprayed for bugs," he said, retrieving the ticket and showing it to her.

She shot a look. No. It didn't explain everything, but it was a start.

Odette took a step toward him and fingered a locket that hung around her neck. She opened it and revealed two pictures. "I was about to show you something before the interruption. The girl on the left is me."

"And the one on the right?"

∽

"THIS IS HER, my half-sister Andie, who I rescued from her father after my mother's death," Odette said. She managed to get the words out before exhaling long and slow.

A look of shock registered.

"She's the reason I needed to take this job," Odette admitted before glancing around. Was it possible her former stepfather planted a listening device somewhere in this apartment? "I don't think we should talk about this any longer while we're here."

Rafe caught on. He gave a little head shake. "What do you need to pick up?"

"My clothes," she said, noting the drawers were at varying degrees of open with garments hanging out. There were pieces on the carpet that had been hastily tossed while someone tore through the apartment with a vengeance.

"I'll wait by the door," Rafe said, catching on immediately to the fact danger might still be present or showing up at any time. They had no idea if there were eyes on the place and she wouldn't put anything past Guy.

Odette packed in a hurry, throwing her garments into a garbage bag for convenience. She raked a hand across the counter in her bathroom, knocking the contents into the bag before pulling on the plastic to cinch the top of the oversized black bag.

"All good?" Rafe asked as he flanked the door, back against the wall. His stance said that anyone who walked through uninvited was about to be shown a whole new exit plan.

Odette nodded as a cramp caused her to take a step back and sit on the bed. She put an arm up. "I'm okay. I just need a minute."

Rafe was by her side before she could take in her next breath, which was unfortunate for her, because when she did all she managed was to breathe his unique musk and spice scent in. Not a good idea being this close to him.

He took the bag from her hand and dropped down to one knee. She pushed the irony of the gesture out of her thoughts as he positioned his elbow next to her on the bed and leaned toward her.

"We can hole up here for as long as you need to," he offered.

"I'll be fine in a few seconds," she reassured, taking in a few slow deep breaths. "Promise."

The worry lines etched in his forehead told her all she needed to know about what kind of father he was going to be. The little bean was going to be in good hands. So, why did she suddenly see herself in the picture?

Shoving the thought down deep, she let him help her to standing.

"All better now," she said.

"Are you sure?" he asked. "Because I don't want you to push it."

The cramp was probably caused by the stress of coming home. Now that she had her personal effects, she wanted to leave.

"Let's get out of here," she said.

He offered an arm, so she took it to steady herself. It would be all too easy to get used to this. Right now, though, was not the time to overanalyze herself. Being pregnant was reason enough to accept help. The fact didn't make her weak or unable to take care of herself.

At the bottom of the stairs, Rafe surveyed the area. She did the same, checking out parked cars to see if anything or anyone inside stirred. Ready at a moment's notice to duck or drop to the concrete. If she didn't need to be around for Andie, she would confront Guy herself. Taking him to court would do no good in Texas, where he had an uncle for a judge. Plus, Odette had gotten into trouble in her late teens, before pulling her life together. Those bad choices would likely haunt her for the rest of her life and could be used against her by a skilled attorney when it came to being awarded custody of Andie.

Once inside the truck, Odette immediately locked her door. She shrank down in the seat and suppressed the urge to scream when the next cramp hit. By the time Rafe reclaimed the driver's seat, the pain was over.

He tossed the bag in the backseat, hit the button to start the engine, and then backed out of the parking spot.

The ride was quiet until they reached the highway headed for Austin.

"Tell me everything," he finally said once they were at a comfortable cruising speed. Considering they were about to be trapped together in a truck for the next seven hours, Odette figured she had no choice but to come clean.

"My half-sister was being neglected and it wouldn't be long before she was physically abused," Odette began. "He was already withholding food to punish her or making her run around the block in the heat, refusing to give her water. I couldn't stand by and do nothing, so I stepped in. The ad for this came in and I took it along with the deposit, and that set Andie up while I finished this assignment."

Rafe sat there, driving, taking it all in with the occasional nod or sympathetic glance in her direction. "I had a feeling you took this job for more pressing reasons than money. Sure, money was important but you had a purpose."

"The way I saw it, and still do, is that we both had something the other one needed," she continued. "For me, that was a way out for my sister. Money was the only option, and I needed a lot fast. For you, it was someone to carry your child."

"Not the easiest way to make money for you," he said.

"No, it isn't," she admitted, cradling the bump. "I honestly didn't expect to feel so attached to this little bean, or care so much what happened to him or her after my part of the job was done. It seemed like it would be so easy to walk away and not look back since the baby doesn't have any of my DNA."

"Except that isn't what is happening," he said for her.

"No, sir. It is not," she confirmed. "But don't think I'm going to go back on the contract. I know what I promised and I'm perfectly capable of following through on my part of the deal. I know what I signed up for and it wouldn't be fair to you to change the rules now because I had no idea how much being the host to this little one might impact my emotions."

"It's understandable," he said after a thoughtful pause. "The way you feel about the kid."

"Even so, I have no plans to do anything about it," she promised. "This is all new to me but I'm a quick study."

"I figured you were, but it's okay to care, Odette."

Those words stopped her cold. Was it? Okay to care? Okay to become attached to something that could never be hers? Okay to want to be in this child's life despite having no blood relation? And okay to have the occasional wish the four of them could be a family?

Odette stopped right there. She'd gone too far. No one made her want to settle down. And that included Mr. Wonderful sitting next to her in the driver's seat. It didn't matter how charming or gorgeous or darn near perfect he seemed to be.

She had plans that didn't involve him. Besides, he was high profile, whereas she had plans to stay on the downlow for the next couple of years. "I have to take care of Andie. She's my only priority and the only person I can afford to care about right now. She has no one but me and I can't let her down."

Why did saying those words out loud suddenly make her feel hollowed out inside?

## 13

Rafe had no plans to talk someone into having any type of relationship with him, be it a casual friendship or something deeper. Plus, his hands were about to be full with a newborn that he had no idea how to take care of by himself. His family still had no idea about the baby and he'd put off dealing with all of it successfully until now. Speaking of family, Odette had spoken up about her former stepfather. She deserved to know about his mother in case the incident from yesterday stemmed from a different source.

"Since we're on the subject of family," he began, thinking they also had a whole lot of time to kill on the road, "you should probably know something about mine."

"Oh yeah?"

"My mother is in jail for attempted murder," he said flat out. He'd never been one to beat around the bush.

Odette gasped.

"I'm sorry," she almost immediately said.

"Don't be," he countered. "She has never been the

warmest individual, and I'm a thousand percent certain she married my dad for money and little else."

"Then, I'm really sorry," she continued. "That must have been difficult growing up."

"My brothers and I were always outside working the ranch," he said, realizing how little he'd interacted with his mother during his youth. "I never really spent a whole lot of time with her over the years. My father was always trying to please her and it never seemed to work, so he had very little time for his boys."

"I will never figure out why some people have children," she said before reaching out to touch his arm. "I didn't mean that to come across as harsh as it did."

"You're right, though," he said. "Not everyone is cut out for the job. My mother is a question mark as to why she decided to have nine children. She says it was to have a girl, but the truth is she was competing with my aunt."

"I can't imagine eighteen boys in one family."

The shock in her voice was comical.

"That's right," he said. Out of the corner of his eye, he saw that she glanced down at the bump. A boy? "I'm guessing you have no clue about the sex of the baby, just like you said before."

"You'd be right," she said. "Can I admit to being curious?"

"Doesn't hurt," he said. "I'd be surprised if you weren't."

"There have been so many nights, especially recently, when I lie awake in bed and wonder what the baby looks like and what sex he or she is," she said. "It's probably just the insomnia and the fact I haven't been working while pregnant. I have, however, finished more crossword puzzles than any one human should ever complete. I've spent hours taking walks and even tried to figure out how to cook. That one didn't go so well. Turns out, I'm better with the microwave and reheating than I am actually trying to cook something." She paused. "I even thought about taking classes once Andie and I are finally together."

Rafe liked the fact she was opening up to him, so he listened.

"I'm not usually this talkative, either," she said as though reading his mind.

"It doesn't bother me," he said. "It's a good way to pass the time on the way home."

"I shouldn't keep talking." Her cheeks flamed. "It's just that I haven't really talked to anyone except this little bean in months."

He didn't think about how lonely and isolating a pregnancy could be, especially since she'd been hiding from someone who sounded like a real jerk. A criminal?

How far would Guy go to find his daughter? To punish Odette? A man like him would have a temper. He clearly didn't respect women. Therefore, had no business bringing up a daughter on his own. Truth be told, Guy didn't need to be around women period. The man should be locked behind bars for the rest of his life or until he could re-learn how to treat the opposite sex. The whole guy's guy act was no excuse for hurting anything smaller and weaker.

"Go ahead," he urged. "I like to hear the sound of your voice." There were other things about her that he liked but this wasn't the right time to go into them. A voice in the back of his head picked that moment to point out the fact he'd never meet anyone who could be so honest, so vulnerable, and so tough all at the same time.

He could almost feel the heat coming off Odette's cheeks from blushing. She didn't take compliments well, deflecting them instead.

Odette cleared her throat. "Since cooking didn't turn out to be my forte, I tried knitting."

He cracked a smile. "How'd that turn out?"

"As badly as you probably expected," she quipped. "I'm not so handy with needles and, turns out, I'm not all that domestic."

"What's that supposed to mean?"

"I can feed myself, but with takeout. I definitely can't sew and I could never see myself as a tennis woman. I need something to do to keep my mind busy," she continued.

"What does interest you?"

"Nature walks turned out to be my solace," she confessed. "If I wasn't about to disappear..." She stopped for a second like she'd caught herself admitting something she was supposed to keep secret. He knew. The jig was up. He just didn't know how he felt about losing her from his and the baby's lives. "Anyway, I wish I could get a dog."

"Really?" he asked. "Somehow I pinned you for a cat person."

"Easy to maintain?"

"Something like that," he admitted.

"You make a good point, except cats don't run up and greet you when you walk in the door," she said. "They also don't bark or keep you safe or go on long walks." Her shoulders relaxed when she spoke. "Plus, I think Andie would really love having a puppy around. It might give her something to look forward to, after being rescued from her home life and taken to a place she'd never been before. She's a sensitive kid and I worry the lack of contact for all this time will affect her. I wonder if she'll even want to see me, or if she'll forget me altogether."

"I doubt that," he said. "I don't see how anyone could forget they knew you."

"Thank you," she responded, sounding a little choked up at the sentiment.

"It's true," he said. "You're remarkable in every way. I'm sure Andie is counting down the days until you pick her up."

Odette sighed. "You have no idea how much I miss that little sprite."

"The feeling is mutual," he reassured. There was no question in his mind. How could anyone who'd met her not remember her vibrancy, her vulnerability? The tough outer shell might be a hard casing but a different side to her lurked underneath. Protective instinct had thickened the walls but when they came down, even for a few minutes, there was nothing but beauty inside and out.

Since he was waxing poetic, he refocused on the stretch of road in front of him. Falling for the surrogate carrying his child wouldn't just be a mistake. It would be a violation of their agreement. Plus, she wasn't exactly asking for anything else from him.

"If you want to know the sex of the baby, we could make a phone call," he said. "With my family's track record, I'm guessing it's a boy."

Odette sat there, contemplating, for a long moment that seemed to stretch out for hours. "As much as I'm curious about the package growing inside me, I'm just a host. I don't have a right to know about the sex. In fact, if you want to be in the delivery room, you can be."

"You didn't want that b—"

"I didn't know you prior to this, did I?" she asked, but it was a rhetorical question. "There's a way to make sure I'm covered up. I spoke to the OB about it in case I changed my mind about having the parent in delivery with me. All you have to do is throw on one of those blue hospital caps along with a pair of scrubs. The nurses will protect my privacy, so I don't end up exposed."

"Are you sure you want that?" he asked, caught off guard when she'd been so adamant about it before. Plus, being together when his child was born might create more of a bond between him and the woman carrying his child. He'd asked the lawyer about it, but the lawyer said it wasn't usually a good idea. Still, he would like to be the first one to hold his child.

"No, but I'm offering anyway because you deserve it," she said. "This is your child with the woman you loved. It seems wrong for the baby not to hear your voice first thing over a doctor and a few nurses. Unless you're uncomfortable with the idea in which case don't worry about it. I'm sure they'll let you stand next to the door or something."

"Who will be in there to help you get through it?" he asked, thinking it wouldn't be fair to leave her alone during something as big as childbirth.

"There will be nurses and a doctor who—"

"I mean, who will be on your team? Telling you to breathe? Or getting ice chips for you?" he asked.

"That's going to be my job," she said. "But don't worry. I've been taking care of myself for a long time. I may not be able to cook but I'm good at keeping myself alive. And, hey, I'm only thirty-two. Maybe cooking won't be my thing until my forties."

She threw out the joke but Rafe didn't laugh. He couldn't smile either. The most monumental thing was going to happen in his life brought about by a woman with no one in her corner, in case the birth became difficult. He couldn't allow that to happen.

"I'd like to be in the room, but as your coach," he said. "Whatever that means."

"We're not too late to take birthing classes together, but it's kind of against the whole point, isn't it?"

"What if the whole point is to bring a healthy baby into the world who is loved by his—"

"Or her—"

"Father," he conceded with a nod. A girl would shatter his world in all the best possible ways. But with Firebrand history behind him, he was most likely going to have a boy.

∽

ODETTE SHOULD ACCEPT THE HELP. Why was it so hard to let someone step in and be her comfort? The short answer? She didn't want to depend on anyone else because she'd been let down too many times in the past to trust.

Wow.

The thought was staggering. Rather than overanalyze it, she shoved the thought down deep and...

Actually, no, she didn't want to gloss over it. "I'd be happy for you to be in the delivery room in any capacity you'd like. Honestly, I've had a few cramps that have knocked me off my backside and I'm more than a little unnerved at what actual labor might feel like, if these things are any indication of how bad it can get."

"Good," he said. "Well, not about being in pain. Thank you for allowing me to be your support. You shouldn't have to go through this alone. And once the baby is born, I'd like to stay in touch. You have taken care of the most precious thing in my life for what will end up being nine months, so I'd like it if the two of you stayed in touch even just a little."

"I guess that would be alright, once Andie and I get settled into our new life," she said. "I might have to disappear for a while, but I should be able to resurface once it's safe for us."

"We'll be at the ranch whenever you're ready to stop by or call," he said.

"I can get your number through the attorney," she stated.

He fished out his cell phone. "Or you could put your information in my contact list right now. For safety's sake, you could make up a name."

"Jennifer Lawrence," she said with a self-satisfied tone.

"Why her?" he asked, remembering how he'd compared her to the actress when they'd first met.

"I don't know," she started. "She appears honest and like the kind of person you want to have a drink after work with. And she's beautiful."

"She doesn't have anything on you," he said under his breath but she was already preoccupied with his cell and must not have heard him. It was probably for the best. He'd promised not to let himself cross another line when it came to Odette, no matter how much his heart argued otherwise. Logically, nothing could happen between the two of them. Logistically, she was about to bolt out of town to disappear. Realistically, he was about to be handed a newborn. Between diapers, work, and taking care of the child, he wasn't going to have time to keep track of anyone else. The two of them staying in touch would be up to her anyway. He wouldn't bother her once she left town no matter how much it would gut him. And it would shred him to pieces.

"Where do you plan to go right after the delivery?" he asked. It was none of his business, but his curiosity got the best of him.

"I have to stick around for a little while at the very least," she said. "Make it through at least one postpartum checkup before I disappear." She was being vague about her next step, which could mean that she didn't have one secured yet.

Could he help her figure it out? Would she allow him to?

"That makes sense," he said. "Have you considered sticking around and fighting?"

"I've come at this from every way possible during the pregnancy," she said. "The idea of me being on the run and hiding out when I've done nothing wrong sticks in my crawl more than I like to admit. Do I want the world to know what a jerk Guy is? Absolutely. But what would that do to Andie?"

She made a point.

"It would hurt her," he admitted. "But so does not having consequences. This person gets to abuse women and nothing happens to him? What message does that send? And who will be around to protect his next target?"

A quick glance said those words struck hard.

Odette's lips formed a thin line and she brought her fist up to prop up her chin, like she did when she was thinking.

"It's easy to get stuck inside your own head, isn't it?" she asked, but the question was rhetorical based on the heavy sigh that came right after. "A person like Guy should be stopped, but at what cost to Andie?"

"The situation isn't an easy one," he agreed. "But if you wanted to stick around and fight, know that you would have my full support."

"As much as I appreciate it, Rafe, and I really do, but being around once the package is delivered might not be my best move," she said in a moment of raw vulnerability. Her hand moved to cover her throat, giving her away.

He couldn't argue her point.

"I just want you to know your options," he said. "There's security at the ranch. You and Andie would be welcome to stay at my house. Me and the baby could move into the main house for a little while. It wouldn't hurt to have family around in those early weeks of taking care of a newborn."

Odette chewed on her bottom lip. Was she considering his offer? Was there hope she wouldn't bolt the minute she could?

"Food could be delivered. Your identity could be kept under wraps until you were ready to emerge," he continued, figuring he was making progress.

A few moments of silence filled the cab. He didn't want to push, so he left her alone to consider his offer.

"Remind me again why you didn't tell your brother Morgan about me and the baby," she finally said.

Damn.

"News spreads like wildfire," he said, realizing he'd just lost all the ground he'd made with her and may never get it back.

## 14

Odette calculated the odds she and Andie could survive without going into hiding. The numbers didn't look good. "I can't risk her life and nothing can happen to me or she has no one."

"Understood," was all Rafe said. The defeat in his tone almost had her reconsidering. "Are you getting hungry?"

"Dinner sounds good," she said, realizing he'd just put up a wall. His body language said he'd tightened up. A growing part of her wanted to ask why, but she knew it would be a mistake to go down the road of attraction and need when she needed to stay focused now more than ever. Odette was getting close to crossing the finish line. And yet, she didn't want to leave the conversation without being completely honest. "I got into trouble when I was younger. It was enough for there to be police reports and probation."

Rafe nodded. "I know."

Did she want to know how? Then again, a person with the kind of money he had would be thorough with an investigation into her background.

"Why did you pick me?" she asked. "If you don't mind my asking."

"You have an honesty about you that made me feel comfortable that you wouldn't hide anything about the pregnancy," he said. "It came across in your video."

"But I wasn't honest about the trouble I'd gotten into," she said.

"People are never black or white," he explained. "We all live in the gray area. You made mistakes more than a decade ago. Why should you have to carry those around for the rest of your life? The last ten-plus years have been rock solid. Plus, I knew you came from what could only be explained as a difficult background. You worked to put yourself through school and made something of yourself. That outweighs mistakes you made when you didn't know better in my book."

"Thank you for trusting me," she said. "Obviously, this money is going to provide a ticket to freedom for me and Andie. There's no way I could have supported her without working for a year or so, while she adjusts to the new reality of living without our mother."

"What you're doing is commendable," he said. "Not many would take on that level of responsibility for another human being or give up their own desires. Most are far too selfish to see past their own nose."

"I'm all she's got," she said by way of explanation.

"Then, Andie is one lucky little girl," he said. Those words spoken by him meant more than she could explain.

"What sounds good for dinner?" he asked, motioning toward the highway sign.

"Something fast, so we don't lose time on the road for the stop, and somewhere that sells salads," she said. "Everything I've been eating lately is giving me heartburn, despite how good it tastes going down."

"That's partially my fault," he said with a small smile, breaking some of the tension. "I've been tempting you with fried foods and ribs. Not exactly food that will calm your stomach."

"Tastes good, though," she said, returning the smile. On a different planet in an alternate universe, she would most definitely fall in love with Rafe Firebrand.

A growing piece of her wondered where the others were. There had to be more like him. Right? Or was that wishful thinking? Because now that she'd gotten to know him, she wouldn't settle for anything less than someone just like him.

"I can find a good salad here," she pointed to a red chicken head logo on an exit sign.

Rafe immediately signaled a lane change before exiting. He pulled into the parking lot. "Do you want to go inside?"

"I'd rather eat in the truck, if that's okay with you," she said. All she needed was to stretch her legs to get the blood flowing again and she'd be good to go.

"Sure," he said. "I just need to hit the bathroom. Do you want to give me your order?"

"I should probably do the same, now that you mention it," she said as he parked.

The pitstop took fifteen minutes and then they were back on the road, heading toward the Austin townhouse. For the rest of the ride, Odette turned onto her side while buckled in and napped.

Rafe's voice startled her awake. She blinked her eyes open. Facing the passenger window, she stilled so she could listen.

"Vaughn and I need to sit down and have a beer," Rafe

said into his phone. "It's the only way to clear the air between us."

"He would be down for that," Morgan said, his voice quiet through the speakers. "I can arrange it."

"Hell, I'll give him a call myself once I'm finished with my business in Austin," he said.

"How long will that take?" Morgan asked.

"A month, give or take," Rafe said.

"That long?"

"I'm afraid so," Rafe confirmed. Was he going to tell his brother about her and the baby? This seemed a good opportunity. "Maybe longer."

"Vaughn and I could take a trip to see you," Morgan offered.

"Not a good idea," Rafe countered.

"Why are you going to be gone so long?" Morgan asked. When his brother got quiet, he said, "Never mind. It's none of my business."

"I'm wrapping up a project that has been taking a while," Rafe said. "You'll know all about it once it's done."

"Okay, cool," Morgan said, sounding confused. "I'll trust you know what you're doing."

The two exchanged goodbyes. Odette couldn't help but feel let down that Rafe hadn't mentioned her or the baby to his brother while he had the chance. This was the second time he could have told Morgan.

She stretched and yawned to let Rafe know that she was awake now.

"Hey," he said. "I hope the phone call didn't wake you up. I tried to be quiet."

"No," she lied. "It didn't."

"Good," he said. "We're about to pull into the garage."

She sat up straight and hit the button to lift her seat back up. The clock on the dashboard read half past eleven.

Her personal life had always been hers. So, why did she suddenly wish Rafe would spill the details of their arrangement to his family? It shouldn't matter to her, considering she wasn't going to be around once the baby was born. And yet, there was something about feeling like she was hiding from everyone that sat heavy on her chest. She was about to disappear. Opening up to someone wasn't in her DNA. Being with Rafe made her question everything she thought she knew about herself and what she wanted in life. Seeing him have roots, despite the hardship his family was facing, made her long for something she'd never allowed herself to want before. Odette had always considered herself more of a free spirit.

Why was that changing now?

∼

"WE NEED TO TALK TO SPENCER," Rafe said after hitting the garage opener. He'd been stewing on the metal button found at Odette's place on the ride home.

"It's obviously too late tonight," Odette pointed out. "Plus, how will we ever get him alone if he's with Kaleb all the time?"

"Good questions," Rafe said. "Let me sleep on it and come up with something in the morning."

He parked in the garage and tapped the button to close the garage door. A hum filled the cab as he cut the engine off. A few seconds later, he was rounding the front of the truck. This time, Odette didn't wait for him to exit the vehicle. She was out and closing the door before he could get there.

Rafe took note, considering she'd been accepting help prior to this. Had he said or done something to offend her?

Rather than ask questions she didn't look ready to answer, he disarmed the alarm and unlocked the door. Odette walked up the stairs and right past him after muttering a goodnight.

Clearly, he'd done something wrong.

Rafe issued a sharp sigh before locking up the house and heading to the guest bathroom. After showering, he went to check on Odette to see if she needed anything or just wanted to talk. Her door was closed and there was no light beaming from underneath the doorway.

Since he didn't sleep much last night, he figured a few hours of shuteye would do him good. He cracked his door and then headed to bed after retrieving her trash bag full of personal effects from the truck. Locking up and setting an alarm were stark reminders of the dangers they faced. Rafe didn't doubt for one second that he could neutralize a threat against him.

But this involved a pregnant woman and his child.

Catching himself grinding his back teeth at the thought, he reminded himself there was nothing else that could be done tonight. A good night of sleep and a fresh cup of coffee normally worked wonders.

Tonight turned out to be the exception. Rafe tossed and turned for the next four hours until he gave up. Ranchers normally started their workday before the sun came up. He shouldn't be surprised his eyes popped open at four a.m. sharp.

He checked his cell phone that he'd placed on the nightstand only to realize he forgot to charge it. The battery had died at some point during the night. Figured.

After a quick bathroom break, he grabbed his cell phone

and headed downstairs. The plug and cable were on the kitchen counter, so he worked his magic before heading over to the coffee machine. He was still full from dinner last night, so he waited for the mug to fill. It didn't take long.

Rafe took the first sip before making a mental checklist of things to do. First and foremost, he needed to speak to Spencer face-to-face. The metal button bothered Rafe. Could it be a coincidence? Sure. And cows could fly.

The question was whether or not Spencer was sent to investigate Odette's home or not. The order could have come from Kaleb while he went into the office. Rafe wasn't sure how to track Spencer's movements since he had no idea if the young man had a job or not at the banking firm where Kaleb worked.

Rafe's cell buzzed as the battery finally got enough charge. The buzzing didn't stop. After another sip of coffee, Rafe headed toward the noise. He checked the screen. There were several texts from Kylie, but his gaze landed hard on one: *Emile's father had a heart attack. He's gone.*

Questions swirled around Rafe's skull, trying to penetrate. How could this have happened? Was it somehow his fault for bringing Odette over to the house yesterday? Had he somehow contributed?

He raked his fingers through his hair and then paced. Although he might not have directly caused the heart attack, it was safe to say Rafe must have contributed. The man looked stressed. His second thought was Kylie didn't need to move out now. She was safe. At least there was one bright spot in the situation. Or was there?

Spencer living at the Cassidy home had never made Emile comfortable. For a split second, Rafe wondered if he should have gone to the police yesterday after finding the metal button. He'd recognized it because Spencer had the shirt on.

Rafe issued a sharp sigh. He sent a text to Kylie with his condolences. She might be relieved on some level but they had a child together and they'd been married for a long time. She wouldn't be human if she didn't feel some sense of loss with Kaleb's passing.

Spencer's button, if that was the case, wouldn't make a hill of beans difference now that Kaleb was gone. Rafe could rule them out moving forward.

Still, he wanted to question Spencer and part of him wouldn't believe the old man was gone without seeing it firsthand. Was that calloused? Probably. But there had never been any love lost between him and Kaleb.

Considering the hour, he was surprised when Kylie sent a thank you text. He set his phone aside to let it fully charge. His thoughts shifted to the other threat in Odette's life, her stepfather. She'd mentioned a first name, Guy. The temptation to put a private investigator on the man's tail was strong. Should he do it without consulting with Odette first?

Would she want him to? Or was he sticking his nose where it didn't belong?

Odette seemed concerned Guy was behind the incident at the restaurant two days ago. Could Rafe request a police report to see what law enforcement decided? The older woman swore she didn't leave her truck in a vulnerable position. But she'd done something similar before and her age could make her forgetful.

Then there was Rafe's own mother to consider. He couldn't rule out the possibility someone was seeking revenge on the family. There'd been death threats since her arrest that no one liked discussing.

Questions swirled as Rafe finished the cup of coffee.

Back to the stairs, he heard wood creak and figured it was Odette coming down. Taking no chances, he closed his fingers around the closest kitchen knife before turning to face the stairwell to the right of the kitchen.

Sure enough, Odette emerged looking sleepy.

"Hey," she said as he released his grip on the blade's handle.

"Morning," he said before adding, "if you can call it that."

Odette rubbed her eyes and cracked a sleepy smile that tugged at his heartstrings. "What's on the agenda today?"

Since bad news only got worse with age, he decided to spit it out. "Kaleb Cassidy had a heart attack."

"What?" she asked, suddenly looking wide awake.

"He died last night."

Odette shook her head. "Something's off."

## 15

Odette didn't like the sound of this news for reasons she couldn't explain. Something niggled at the back of her mind. What?

If only she could have a cup of coffee to clear the cobwebs. Going without hadn't done her any favors in the quick-thinking department. "Where was he? How did it happen?"

Rafe stood shirtless in the kitchen for a long moment. Odette's gaze dropped to his chiseled chest where ripples of muscles formed an impossible V. His body was perfection. She flexed and released her fingers a couple of times to stop from reaching out to touch him. The man's body was sex on a stick with his clothes on. Without, he only got better.

This wasn't the right time to think about the brief kiss they'd shared. Or the fact her lips burned for a repeat.

"I don't have all the details," he admitted, breaking into her thoughts. "I was thinking we might want to swing by their home again this morning. I'd still like to ask Spencer a few questions."

"Same here," she agreed, refocusing her attention on her growling stomach. "I need to eat something first and..." She glanced at the clock. "It's a little too early for the drive over."

"Kylie is awake," he said. "But I agree. I highly doubt Spencer is."

"That'll give me time to wake up and process this news," she said. "The man might have been a jerk and deserved to be put behind bars but I can't wish death on anyone."

Odette walked over to the fridge and grabbed a yogurt. On the counter, she picked up a banana. Milk rounded out the meal. The sausage from yesterday's breakfast scramble might have tasted amazing as it went down the pipe, but she'd felt it burn her throat the rest of the day.

Rafe's muscles were on full display on his shirtless torso. He held up a hand before disappearing upstairs and returning with more clothing on.

The small breakfast kept her stomach calm. The smell of coffee used to make her sick to her stomach in the early months despite being an almost lifelong drinker of fresh brew. Now? She missed the taste and the energy boost that came along with it. In those early months, she'd been too sick to focus on what she was missing. Now, she would give her right arm for a glass of wine or an iced latte.

Funny how easy it was to focus on mundane things rather than dwell on the fact the baby's grandfather was dead. Odette could only imagine what Kylie must be feeling. Remorse? Regret? Guilt?

She polished off the banana before grabbing an apple and finishing the milk.

"How did you sleep?" Rafe asked, fixing a cup of coffee. Was it his second? Third?

"Better," she admitted. "It seems like I can only grab four

or five hours at one time these days on a good night. Last night definitely classified as one of the best."

"That's good to hear."

"I'm guessing it wasn't the same for you," she said.

"Not exactly but I can get by on a couple hours of sleep without a whole lot of trouble," he explained. "During calving season, it's not uncommon for ranchers to go two to three days without more than fifteen minutes of shuteye here and there."

"Sounds awful," she said, making a face.

He laughed. "You get used to it."

"Do you get along with your brothers?" she asked, wanting to know more about him while they waited for a decent hour before heading out.

This time, he chuckled. It lit up his whole face. "Depends on the day."

"I'm being serious," she said. "I grew up as an only child. I was twenty-five by the time my sister was born." She palmed the apple. "I always wanted to be from a big family growing up. I fantasized about it all the time. Sisters and brothers running around everywhere in a home with two parents. The smell of cookies baking on Christmas, wafting through the house."

"I might have had two parents, but that didn't necessarily mean I came from a happy home," he pointed out. "And those big family Christmases were in short supply since my mother always seemed to be in competition with my aunt, who is the most salt-of-the-earth type. She's the kind who made homemade meatballs for all of us. She never made us feel less than for coming from the other side of the family. Of course, we became teenagers and lines were drawn between families but that's all water under the bridge now."

"It seems like you're close with Morgan," she said.

"True." He grabbed his coffee mug and took a sip. "My brother Vaughn and I have the real beef. The stupid thing about it all is that I don't even remember how it all started. But I do recall the big fight that ended all communication."

"Let me guess," she said, "a girl."

"No, but that's why one of my brothers and one of my cousins had a falling out," he said. "This was over who was the most valuable basketball player in high school."

"You don't get along with your brother over a sport?" she asked.

Rafe shrugged. "We disagreed on most things growing up. Vaughn threw an elbow into my eye while going for a ball in what was supposed to be a friendly game with our teammates after practice. I ended up with four stitches at my eyebrow line." He moved closer and pointed out the scar.

She resisted the urge to run her finger along the raised skin.

"Clearly, it was more than basketball," he said. "We went after each other every chance we got. I guess we were always competitive with each other for some reason."

"Sibling rivalry," she said.

"Looking back, we were just a couple of hotheads with too much testosterone and not enough common sense," he admitted. "Funny thing is, the whole rivalry started as just friendly teasing between us that somehow escalated during what were supposed to be friendly matchups."

"Seems like it's high time to put the past behind the two of you and start a new chapter as grown men," she said.

"I couldn't agree more." He took a sip of coffee. "Strange how competitiveness can fester and turn into something bad. Our grandfather was the master at pitting my father against his brother. Their rivalry lasted until my grandfather's death and the family is just now beginning to heal. Well, at least until my mother pulled what she did. Now, I wouldn't blame the other side of the family for never talking to us again."

"It never occurred to me that bigger families could mean more complications," she said. "In my image, everyone gets along Norman Rockwell style. It's naïve, isn't it."

"No," he said after a thoughtful pause. "It's actually sweet. I have to believe a strong family can be built, if parents instill those values in their children."

"Would you consider having more children?" she asked.

His expression turned serious. She regretted the question almost the minute it left her mouth.

"You don't have to answer that," she said. "It was insensitive of me. The woman you'd planned to spend the rest of your life with is gone. This baby is a miracle as it is. Of course, you don't want to have any additional children."

"I might," he said. "If the right person came along and had the same mindset."

Odette refused to read too much into the statement. Because there was no way he was talking about her, despite her heart trying to convince her of just that. A heart that betrayed her into thinking a real relationship might be possible with an honest man like Rafe. He had all the qualities she could ask for in a life partner; loyalty, intelligence, honor. All of those traits were wrapped in one seriously hot package.

"What about you?" he asked. "You're planning to take care of your half-sister. Do you ever consider having a family at some point?"

She shook her head. "It's just going to be me and Andie."

~

Rafe would tell her that her future sounded lonely, except it would make him the biggest hypocrite in Texas. Then again, he never expected to meet anyone like her. She was stubborn and smart, and yet there was a vulnerable side to her that drew out all of his protective instincts. Instincts that made him want to stick around long after the baby was born to explore a relationship with Odette.

"I better go get ready," Odette said, ending the conversation on that note. She headed upstairs as he finished his second cup of coffee.

At this point, he was ready to eat so he heated a premade meal and polished it off. Sitting at the counter, he felt lonely. It was strange because Odette was right upstairs and he hadn't felt this kind of empty in more years than he could count.

To be perfectly honest, there were times during his relationship with Emile that he felt this way with her in the room. With Odette, it was different. Was it because she was carrying his child? Or something else? Something he hadn't allowed himself to feel since losing Emile?

Shaking off those thoughts, he headed upstairs to throw on a sweater. A cold front was moving through this morning despite an abundance of sunshine.

By the time he tinkered around in the guest bedroom and headed downstairs, it was time to head out.

"Thank you for bringing my bag upstairs," Odette said as she sat perched on the barstool, waiting for him.

"Not a problem," he said as he grabbed keys and toed on his boots. "Ready?"

Odette had on a skirt with a sweater. She might have commented about how huge she looked, but the bump wasn't much more than the size of a basketball. Her skin had a glow that made her even more attractive.

She slipped on flats and followed him out to the truck.

Rafe had the distinct feeling he was going to miss Odette more than he wanted to acknowledge when their transaction was over with. But right now, he needed to figure out what Spencer was up to.

One more thing.

"You mentioned your stepfather might have been responsible for the diner incident," he said. "Do you have a picture of him? It would be nice to know who he was if I saw him coming at me."

"Right," she said, pulling her cell phone out of her handbag. After securing seatbelts, she held out her screen.

"Blond hair and blue eyes," he said. "Got it."

"He's not as tall as you are," she said. "He can't be more than five-feet-ten-inches."

"Good to know," he said. "Do you have a guess as to his weight? It's hard to tell in pictures."

"I'd say he isn't more than a hundred and sixty pounds," she informed. "But that's just a guess. I know he likes to check himself out in the mirror all the time. There wasn't one that he walked past that he didn't stop to flex in front of. And he has a tattoo of a snake wrapped around a motorcycle on his bicep."

"Got it," he confirmed, making a mental note of the details just in case he needed them.

After hitting the garage button, he started the engine. Doors were locked and the alarm was set. They were good to go.

The drive to the Cassidy home took about the same amount of time as it did yesterday. Kylie opened the door almost the second they knocked. Big crocodile tears rolled down her face as she practically threw herself into Rafe. He gave her a hug before reaching for Odette's hand.

After linking their fingers, he followed Kylie inside the home.

"I can't apologize enough for Kaleb's behavior toward both of you yesterday," Kylie began as she took a seat at the marble island. She had a delicate cup that she was drinking coffee out of and Rafe was almost one hundred percent certain there was something stronger in that cup than caffeine. "He really was a better man than that."

Based on their conversation yesterday, this was quite an about-face.

"We stopped by to ask Spencer a few questions," Rafe stated after telling Kylie how sorry they were for her loss.

"Spence?" she asked, eyebrow raised. "What does he have to do with anything?"

There was a strangely defensive note in her tone. Why was she suddenly being defensive of Spencer? Loss did odd things to people, so he decided not to put too much stock in it until Odette's grip tightened around his fingers.

"I was hoping to have a conversation with him," was all Rafe said by way of explanation.

"Well, you can't because he's not here," Kylie said, her voice raising a couple of octaves. "He didn't come home last night after losing Kaleb. He's at the funeral home because he didn't want to leave his uncle alone."

Kylie straightened her back and took a sip from her cup.

"What time do you expect him?" Rafe asked.

"I really don't know," Kylie said. "What could you possibly want with him?"

"I'd rather speak to him directly, if you don't mind," Rafe continued.

"I kind of do mind," Kylie defended.

Just as Kylie's shoulders squared as though ready for a fight, Spencer came walking down the back staircase and into the kitchen. His hair was messy and he shot a dirty look at Rafe. The young man looked like he hadn't slept in a week.

Kylie was either naïve or intentionally protecting Spencer. Rafe had no idea which one but intended to find out for her own protection. He reached into his pocket and pulled out the button he'd put there. He held it flat on his palm.

"Are you missing something?" he asked Spencer pointedly.

The young man glanced at the button and practically sneered. "No. Why? Should I be?"

How old was Spencer now? He had to be in his early twenties.

"I seem to remember the button is a match."

Spencer held up his wrist. "Most shirts have buttons, so..."

Rafe had to hold back from dressing down the insulant snit. Spencer had the attitude that came with what he was... a prep school dropout. Or should Rafe say someone who'd been kicked out of several fancy private schools?

"Funny because I distinctly remember the button. How about you show me the shirt you had on yesterday," Rafe hedged.

Spencer shot him a go-to-hell look.

"The past twenty-four hours have been hard on everyone, so I think we should just stop right here," Kylie said, waving her arms in the air. She had on a push-up bra that highlighted her ample chest and her hoodie was zipped low enough for the 'girls' to peek out. Was this the outfit of a grieving woman? It seemed a little too revealing, but then Rafe wasn't here to judge.

Rafe couldn't help but wonder if the visit yesterday was responsible for the heart attack or the alcohol on Kylie's breath.

Or was something else going on entirely?

## 16

Odette stood quietly, taking in the scene unfolding in front of them. She had a deep desire to get the hell out of there. Spencer wasn't acting right. Kylie seemed like a different person today. Grief did strange things to folks. Odette knew firsthand how lost someone could feel after losing a loved one. She didn't wish that nightmare on anyone.

This whole scene creeped her out though. She wanted to leave.

"Where were you last night?" Rafe asked Spencer.

"Here," Spencer responded.

A look passed between Kylie and Spencer that Odette caught. What was going on between those two? Were they bonded in loss? Still reeling?

"You should probably go," Kylie said to Rafe. "Come back another time."

Rafe opened his mouth to protest, but Odette squeezed his hand in the hopes he wouldn't. They needed to leave well enough alone. Besides, she had a bad feeling being here and wanted to get out as soon as possible.

"We'll be back to check on you," Rafe said to Kylie.

"Okay," she responded. "I appreciate it."

Somehow, Odette doubted Kylie wanted either one of them inside the house. What did she think they would do?

Once back inside the truck, Rafe issued a sharp sigh. "That was by far the most bizarre meeting I've ever had with the Cassidy family."

"People grieve differently, so I don't want to overstep my bounds here," she said. "But, there wasn't anything normal about what we just experienced."

"Everything was off, right?" Rafe asked as he backed out of the drive. He navigated onto the roadway, checking the rearview mirror as though afraid someone might follow them.

"I'm not sure how we went from Kylie talking about being abused yesterday and needing to get out to her protecting Spencer today," she admitted.

"You caught onto that too?" Rafe said. "I was beginning to believe I was the crazy one."

"Whatever is going on in that house made me want to run," Odette said. "My hormones are way too off to be so uncomfortable."

"Spencer is hiding something," Rafe said. "I can feel it."

"Are you sure he isn't just mourning the loss of an uncle who took him in when he had nowhere else to go?" she asked, figuring it was good to cover all the bases.

"It would be nice if that was the case," he continued. "I highly doubt it."

"Same here," she admitted. "I was just dotting every i and crossing every t."

"I don't know what Spencer is up to, but I sure would like to see the coroner's report on Kaleb," Rafe said.

"Cardiac arrest isn't the most surprising thing," she said.

"It's almost too neat of an explanation," he said before issuing another sharp sigh. "I don't know how to explain it, but I'm concerned about foul play."

"Kaleb has a high stress job," she said, playing devil's advocate. "He was disturbed by our presence yesterday."

"True," Rafe agreed. As he pulled into the townhouse drive, he hit the brake.

A squad car was waiting in front of their townhouse.

"What now?" he asked before pulling into the garage.

The minute they stepped inside the townhouse, the doorbell rang.

"Do you want to go upstairs?" he asked.

"No," she said, "I'm interested in what they have to say."

Rafe answered the door, failing to invite the officer inside. "How can I help you, sir?"

"May I come in?" the officer asked.

"We can do this right here," Rafe responded, standing his ground.

The man introduced himself as Officer Smith. Rafe extended a hand, which the officer took.

"Are you Rafe Firebrand?" Officer Smith asked.

"Yes, sir," Rafe responded.

"Did you visit the home of Kaleb Cassidy yesterday?" Officer Smith asked.

"Yes, sir," came the response.

"And did you notice there was anything unusual about Kaleb Cassidy when you visited?" Officer Smith continued.

Odette stood off to the side, praying the officer didn't ask for her name in case Guy had reported Andie as missing and given Odette's information as a suspect. She'd scoured the internet in those early days after taking her half-sister, searching for signs she'd been reported. Guy had a lot to lose if his actions came to light. Would he still get custody of

Andie? Would he be able to force Odette out of the little girl's life? Those were questions Odette couldn't afford to get the wrong answers to.

"No, sir."

"Can you describe Kaleb Cassidy's general state?" Officer Smith asked.

"He seemed agitated by my visit," Rafe explained in as few words as possible.

"How so, if you don't mind my asking," the officer continued.

"I'd just delivered the news that his daughter, who has been dead for five years, is about to have a child with me," Rafe stated. "How do you think he took the news?"

The officer's eyebrow shot up as he took notes.

After a few routine-sounding questions, the officer thanked them for their time before excusing himself. Odette stood at the doorway, watching as the squad car pulled away.

"We need to visit your stepfather to get a baseline on where he stands with you," Rafe said.

Odette closed the door, and then locked it. "I'm not going to his home."

"Where does he work?" he asked. "Going to his place of employment might be safer anyway."

"He's the manager at AutoFix," she supplied. "But, I'm not sure it's safe for me to confront him."

"I'll be there, right by your side," he said with the kind of protectiveness that made her believe he meant every word. "He can't hurt you."

Odette needed answers. Would this bring some?

"Okay," she conceded, gathering up her purse before she could get comfortable. "Let's go."

Every emotion struck on the ride over from fear to indignation to relief that she might live out these last couple of weeks in peace. The growing threat had her nerves on edge, which wasn't good for her or the pregnancy. Could they shut it down with one visit?

Bullies needed to be backed down. Guy was a bully. If Andie wasn't involved, Odette would have no problem backing the man down and then walking out of his life forever. However, Andie would get caught up in the middle and Odette wanted better for her half-sister. Rafe was the opposite of the men Odette had grown up around. There was no question he got angry. But he maintained control over his temper, never losing it or degrading someone out of anger.

There should be more men like Rafe Firebrand.

～

RAFE PULLED into the parking lot at AutoFix. He rounded the front of the vehicle to help Odette out of the passenger side when a man came barreling across the lot. He recognized Guy immediately from the picture and description.

Rafe stiff-armed Guy as Odette climbed out of the truck. "Hold on there, buddy. Where do you think you're going?"

Odette stood at the opened truck door, frozen.

"Where is she?" Guy shouted. "Where's my daughter?"

"Look at me," Rafe said calmly, redirecting the man's anger, as another worker exited the building and made a beeline toward them. "Ask me."

Guy's gaze bounced from Rafe to Odette and back.

"Is she safe?" he finally asked as the second uniformed man joined them.

Guy's body trembled. Rafe had no idea if it was from anger, fear, or both. And then he broke down into tears.

"Hey, buddy," the second man comforted. "It's going to be alright." He kept a distance from Rafe. Was he scared?"

"She's okay," Odette said, not budging an inch.

"Where is she?" he asked as his gaze searched the vehicle.

"Not here," Odette stated.

"Who are you?" Rafe asked the second man.

"I'm Billy and I'm Guy's sponsor," Billy supplied. He put a hand up. "We don't want any trouble, but if you folks would like to come inside, we can have a cup of coffee and talk in my office.

The word *sponsor* didn't go unnoticed by Rafe. It was clear Billy didn't say *supervisor*. A sponsor likely meant one thing, Alcoholics Anonymous. Was Guy getting sober?

"It would mean a lot if we could sit down and work through this together," Billy continued.

Rafe deferred to Odette, who gave a slight nod.

"Why don't the two of you go inside first and we'll join you in a few minutes," Rafe offered, needing to make certain Odette was comfortable with the arrangement.

"Does that sound good?" Billy asked Guy.

"Promise you'll come inside?" Guy asked Rafe in an almost helpless voice.

"I will, but I can't speak for Odette," Rafe promised. "We won't leave without warning."

"We can live with that," Billy said before escorting Guy across the parking lot and back into the building.

"What do you think?" Rafe asked as soon as the pair was out of earshot. He walked over to Odette and, consequences be damned, wrapped his arms around her, bringing her into an embrace.

"We have a lot of history that is holding me back," she said. "But I heard the word sponsor being used and that makes me think Guy might be trying to change, which makes me conflicted."

Rafe listened as she worked through it all in her mind.

"They say that everyone deserves a second chance," she conceded. "I'm just still so angry at him for the way he treated my mother that I don't know if I can get past it."

"No one would blame you if you couldn't," he said, and meant it. In his heart of hearts, though, he didn't see her as the kind of person who could live with herself if she didn't at least try. "You can go at your own pace. You don't owe him or anyone else anything."

"I owe it to Andie," she said quietly. "She is the one who ends up hurt the most by not having at least one parent in her life if, and only if, he can get his life together and keep it that way."

"She has you," he pointed out.

"And what if something happens to me?" she asked. "Who would she have then?"

"Those are good points," he agreed.

"I guess we're going inside then," she said after taking in a long, slow breath.

"In case no one has told you this, Odette," he started. "You are a very special person." He didn't add the words *to me*, no matter how much he wanted to. He had suspicions that she felt the same way about him but no confirmation or reason to believe she was prepared to act on them.

"It means a whole lot more coming from you," she said so quietly he almost didn't hear her.

His chest squeezed and he knew right then and there how much trouble he was in with Odette. There was a point of no return when it came to feelings and he stood on the line. Think about her much more and there'd be no going back.

Funny thing was, he didn't want to shut down his thoughts about her. And he wasn't certain he could even if he wanted to.

Reaching for her hand, he linked their fingers before walking into the repair shop. There was only one office, to the right, and the door was cracked. The window was tinted but he could see a figure pacing on the other side.

Taking the lead, he walked them to the door and then knocked.

"Come in," Billy said.

Rafe took a step inside, expecting Odette to position herself behind him. She surprised him when she let go of his hand and walked around him.

Folding her arms across her chest, she began, "I don't want to hear apologies or excuses, Guy. We both know what you put my mother through. But if you're honest about wanting to change, I'll listen."

Guy broke down in tears as he gripped the mug.

For one thing, Rafe could rule the man out when it came to the incident at the diner, if that wasn't the accident folks claimed it to be.

"I've been sober now for five months, fourteen days, and…" He glanced at the ticking clock on the wall, "six hours."

Billy nodded to confirm.

"Why now?" she asked.

"Because I had to hit rock bottom before I could face facts," he said. "I'm an alcoholic. In recovery now, but I have a lot to make up for."

Odette's body language relaxed slightly. "It's good that you're committed to changing."

"I am," he promised, taking another sip of coffee. "I have a long way to go."

"Then you won't mind the fact that I have no plans to return Andie to you until you've proven this can last," she said, her voice a study in calm.

"No, but I am her father and I would like to see her," he stated, his gaze fixed on her belly.

"If you stay on this path, that won't be a problem," Odette said. "She's away right now in a safe place, where she's being cared for."

"You aren't married? She isn't living with you?" Confusion drew his eyebrows together.

"There's a lot you don't know, and this isn't the time to explain," she stated. "You're going to have to trust that I know what I'm doing."

"Can I speak to her on the phone at least?" he asked.

"It can be arranged," Odette said. "But I need reassurances first."

"Like?"

"You have to be sober for a year," she insisted. "Minimum."

Guy was already shaking his head no. "Too long."

Odette stared at him for a long moment. "You do this right and you'll have your daughter for the rest of your life. Mess it up, and you'll never see her again. Now, I have good reason not to trust you, but I hope for Andie's sake that you stick to whatever it is you're doing. I *want* her to have a relationship with her father because it's good for her in the long run. But only if it's healthy and, for a long time in the future, supervised."

He took in a deep breath.

"You're right," he said. "I need to prove that I've changed. But how?"

"We can talk weekly and I'd like to check in with your

sponsor," she said. "If things go well, we'll adjust the timeline for you and Andie to speak on the phone."

"Okay," Guy conceded after checking with Billy, who gave a quick nod of approval. "That's fair."

Like Odette said, everyone deserved a second chance in life, but no one had a right to one. She was being more than fair. And, if he knew her like he believed he did, she would revise the timeline once she saw Guy was committed to his recovery.

A person like Odette didn't come around often.

## 17

Odette walked out of the auto repair shop feeling the most optimistic she had in longer than she could remember. Don't get her wrong, she planned to be cautious with Guy. But he wasn't behind the break-in and seemed committed to change. Only time would tell. She slid into the passenger seat and secured her seatbelt as Rafe reclaimed the driver's side.

"We can rule him out as someone who would be snooping around my apartment or tracking me at the diner," she said once Rafe navigated onto the roadway.

"I had the same thought while we were still inside," he said. "Five months of sobriety is a start toward healing."

"As much as I want to believe it's true and bring Andie home, I have to be cautious for her sake," she explained. "I can't expose her to the kind of behavior that he previously displayed. Ever. He crossed too many lines when he drank too much."

"True," he said. "That's exercising good judgment on your part."

"I also believe in second chances, but I'll be taking it

slow in this case," she continued, grateful to have someone to bounce her thoughts off of.

He nodded.

"Where are we headed now?" she asked, biting back a yawn.

"Home," he said, like this wasn't a temporary setup and the two of them weren't going their separate ways once the baby was born.

Odette reminded herself not to get too comfortable. Did they have a connection? Yes. It was undeniable at this point to her, him, and probably everyone around them. Was there chemistry? Absolutely. It sizzled every time their skin came into contact. Could this go anywhere?

She stopped herself right there. A relationship wasn't on the table. Period.

Besides, there was still someone out there who seemed intent on either spying on her or hurting her or both. This wasn't a good time for a distraction. In fact, it could have deadly consequences.

Odette closed her eyes and tried to process the changes in Guy. He appeared genuine and it really would be in the best interest of Andie if her father was around on some level. She sighed in relief because there wasn't a day that went by she didn't wish for more time with her mother. Andie had already lost one parent.

Lost in thought, Rafe was pulling into the garage back at the townhouse before she knew it. He closed the door behind them and cut the engine. He helped her climb down from the passenger seat before realizing they'd forgotten to set the alarm.

Rafe brought his index finger to his mouth, made eye contact, and then tucked Odette behind him. He climbed the stairs, taking one at a time, careful not to make a sound as she followed.

Hand on the doorknob leading to the kitchen, a door slam sounded from inside the townhouse. Odette's pulse skyrocketed as Rafe bolted inside.

She took a couple of steps inside and caught sight of the miniblinds swaying from across the room. Someone was in the house. Rafe gave chase as she reached for a chopping knife.

"Stay back, call 911, and stay alert," he instructed as he bounded across the space. Not three seconds later, he disappeared.

Heart pounding, Odette reached inside her purse for her cell phone while surveying the room. It occurred to her more than one person might be inside. The runner could be a distraction.

Backing up against the wall in the corner where she had the best vantage point, she quickly made the 911 call. She set the phone down on the counter while staying on the line after spitting out the emergency. This way, she could call out a description if there was someone in the house.

*Stay calm* was her mantra. She wasn't concerned about herself so much as what would happen to Andie if Odette was killed. Not to mention the baby inside her. Odette instinctively wrapped her free arm around her belly as she kept the knife ready to go in her right hand.

Taking a step forward to investigate, she came around the side of the granite island. A noise like a rattle startled her. And then before she could react, a snake lurched toward her.

Odette screamed and jumped.

She threw the chunky knife at its head, nailed it, knocking it to the side. The knife landed with a hard thud.

Before the rattler could regroup, she turned tail and bolted around the granite island toward the back door. Running through the kitchen, she turned right and ran down to the garage.

Realizing she didn't have keys and unable to stay inside the townhouse alone for another second, she opened the garage door. After hitting the button one more time, she ducked and ran without tripping the sensor.

∽

Rafe turned the corner at full speed. The jerk who'd broken into the townhouse had too much of a head start, and was a fast runner to boot. Still, Rafe had no plans to stop. His thighs burned and his lungs clawed for air but he kept pushing. He could see an occasional glimpse of the runner, who wore light jeans and a dark hoodie.

His first inclination was this had to be Spencer based on the guy's size but Rafe doubted he could run this fast. Then again, a spike of adrenaline could work wonders.

His second thought had to do with his mother's actions. Could this break-in be tied back to her? Did someone want revenge? No one else in the family was being targeted as far as he knew. But that didn't mean the person wouldn't start with Rafe or didn't have other plans in the works for the others.

Rafe zigzagged through the townhouses as he tried to keep pace. The runner hopped onto the hood of a sedan before jumping the concrete wall surrounding the complex. The car's alarm pierced the air, splitting Rafe's head in two.

He climbed onto an air conditioning unit instead before hopping over the wall and into a neighborhood. A quick glance left and then right, Rafe quickly realized he'd lost visual contact with the runner.

Biting back a curse, he stayed put as he heaved for air and waited for any sign of the runner.

Dammit.

Rafe lost the guy. He released a string of curse words underneath his breath as he brought his hands up, elbows out and then clasped his fingers over his head. He'd learn the trick a long time ago that opened up the chest to take in more air.

From the corner of his right eye, he caught glimpse of someone darting around a house. Rafe cut right and aimed in the runner's direction. The guy was already six or seven houses down, and about to have access to a road. The wide-open space might make it easier to keep tabs while Rafe pushed his legs to run faster.

The best he could do was close the distance between them by a few feet by the time the runner made the corner. From there, he could continue straight, which was unlikely, or wind through another maze of houses.

If Rafe couldn't push a little harder, there was no way he was going to bridge the gap between them.

By the time he reached the road, more sirens cut through the air. This familiar sound belonged to the law. Help was on the way. Was it too late?

Rafe ran down the street and back, checking each possible turn off point. He opened garbage bin lids as he circled back toward the townhouse. Leaving Odette alone for too long caused more waves of panic to wash over him.

By the time he got to the townhouse, there was a police vehicle out front and a pair of officers walking toward the door.

"Excuse me," he said to them as he gasped for air. "This is my home. I asked my friend to call in an emergency."

The male and female officers turned around simultaneously.

"I'm Officer Parker," the female said before turning to her partner. "This is Officer Miles."

Rafe noticed both officers kept their right hands over the butt of their weapons.

"Rafe Firebrand," he said to them both through labored breaths. "I just chased a guy in light jeans and a dark hoodie that way." He pointed toward the wall. "He's fast."

"Did you get a look at his face, by chance?" Officer Parker asked.

Rafe shook his head. "My friend who made the call to 911 is still inside and I'm concerned about her safety." He started toward the front door.

"Hold on, sir," Officer Parker said, taking a step back. "My partner and I have a couple of questions first."

"She might be in trouble," he stated, turning to go around them. "She would be outside by now otherwise."

Officer Parker spoke into her radio before following Rafe.

"This is your home, sir?" Officer Parker said from behind as he took the steps two at a time.

"Yes, ma'am," he confirmed as he approached the door that was still ajar. "Odette."

A cold chill raced down his spine when there was no response.

"I'm going inside," Rafe said to the officers.

"Sir, I don't advise do—"

He didn't stick around long enough to hear the rest of the officer's sentence. She could do what she wanted to. He was going in.

Rafe took a couple of steps inside and called out to Odette one more time. *Dammit.*

All kinds of horrific images assaulted his brain. In many of them, Odette was tied to a piece of furniture and gagged, rendering her unable to respond. In others, she was incapacitated, unconscious, or too weak to yell. Another haunting picture had someone's hand over her mouth as she tried to breathe.

Clearing the first floor became his first priority. "I'll check closets down here if the two of you want to move forward. There's a garage downstairs and bedrooms up."

"I'll take down," Officer Parker said to her partner. At least there was some relief in knowing Rafe would have help. Three of them could cover more ground faster, and that might mean the difference between life and death for Odette and the baby. As much as he needed the baby to be okay, the thought of anything happening to Odette because of him nearly gutted him.

The thought he could lose her forever was a sucker punch to the solar plexus.

Rafe sucked in a breath as he and the officers fanned out. Running right, he heard a familiar-sounding rattle near the granite island. "Everybody freeze."

"What's that noise?" Officer Parker asked as her partner put a hand out to stop her from moving forward. Officer Miles took a step back.

"Rattler," he said.

"Uncommon in these parts," Rafe stated. He was a little too familiar with them on the family ranch. Considering the fact they crawl around five miles per hour, he wasn't scared of racing one. It was the strike he had to watch out for. Those came faster than his brain could process until the pit vipers were midair.

Rafe realized immediately the rattler had been planted. There was no reason for it to be inside someone's home. On the porch, sunbathing during winter months, yes. But not inside a home where there was no hot deck or concrete.

"I'll make a call," Officer Miles said.

"We don't have time for Animal Services," Rafe stated. "Distract it while I whip around the other side of the granite."

Before Officer Miles could protest, Parker started waving her hands in the air. She took a couple of steps in the opposite direction of Rafe, which he appreciated. Now, he needed to find something to snatch the snake with and something else to put it inside.

After grabbing kitchen tongs that weren't nearly long enough for his comfort, he said, "Grab the couch cushion covers and make a thick bag with them, inserting one inside the other to double up."

Officer Miles caught on. With a quick nod, he made a beeline for the sofa. After unzipping and then pulling out the foam stuffing, he jogged over. "You catch that thing and drop it in, I'll make sure it stays inside here."

"Much appreciated," Rafe said before creeping around back of the granite island. He was keenly aware of the fact Odette could be hurting and every second could mean life or death.

Adrenaline thumped in his ears like a drumbeat.

Go too fast and the snake could track him. Go too slow and Odette could be in worse trouble. Anger ripped through him as he moved with a steady rhythm toward the rattler. The pit viper was agitated as Officer Parker clapped her hands toward it.

Rafe couldn't think. He had to act.

Now.

He reached for the snake's body, several inches down it's neck. With a steady hand, he caught it on the first try, clamping the tongs tight so it couldn't jerk out of its grip.

Officer Miles came around back in the next second, bag open. Rafe immediately set the angry rattler inside the bag as the officer held it away from his body.

While Rafe held still, the officer zipped the cushion, locking the snake inside. Rafe pulled out the tongs to close the zipper. Officer Miles tossed the bag onto the floor and took a giant step back.

Just as Rafe turned to resume searching for Odette, the front door opened and she stood there.

"It's okay," Rafe reassured as Officer Parker drew her weapon. "This is Odette. This is the person I already told you about. This is who we were about to search for."

Officer Parker holstered her weapon before speaking into the radio clipped to her shoulder. Rafe didn't pay attention to what the officer said. He was already halfway across the room.

"You're safe," he said to Odette.

"So are you," she pointed out, bending over and touching her back.

"Come inside," he said to her. "Sit down on the chair while we check the rest of the house."

"We got this," Officer Parker said, holding out his hand.

"Where have you been?" he asked Odette.

"The snake," she said through labored breaths.

"Are you okay? Is something wrong?" he asked, scared out of his mind she was going into labor.

"I'm good," she quickly reassured. "Just out of breath."

Rafe exhaled.

"I panicked when the snake jumped at me," she continued. She locked onto his gaze. "I'm guessing the guy got away."

He nodded.

"The place is clear," Officer Parker said as she came down the stairs. Her partner joined her from the garage. "We'll take that from you."

"Yes, please, get it out of here," Odette said.

"We'll just need to get your statements," Officer Parker said. "And then we'll be around, canvasing the neighbors. Maybe one of them saw something."

"Thank you, officers," Rafe said before taking turns giving their statements to the officers.

Once the snake was removed from the premises, Odette relaxed a little more.

"That was strange," she said once the officers were gone. "A rattler on the inside of a home doesn't ring true to me."

"I thought the same thing," he admitted, glancing into the kitchen area and noticing the pantry door was ajar. "Did you notice that before?"

"What?" she asked.

He pointed to the opened door.

"No, I didn't," she said as his cell buzzed. He fished it out of his pocket and checked the screen. "It's Kylie. She's asking us to come right away with a request that we park the truck down the street, so Spencer isn't alerted to our arrival."

"That doesn't sound good," Odette stated with concerned eyes.

"She wants us to come through the garage," he said, thinking the exact same thing. Spencer couldn't be in two places at once. Was he home?

Rafe was about to find out.

## 18

Odette did her best to keep her nerves as far below panic as possible on the drive over to Kylie's. After the break-in and snake incident at the townhouse, she didn't want to stay there alone. The officers had promised to call if and when they picked up the runner. No call had come in thus far, so he was still out there somewhere.

Rafe parked the truck four houses down, as requested. He came around the front of the vehicle to open Odette's door and then help her down. The second her feet hit concrete, she reached up and hugged him. The hug had a calming effect on her. She steeled her nerves further by taking in a slow breath.

"I'm ready now," she said to him, realizing how quickly he'd become her lifeline.

"Okay," he said, his voice low and gravelly.

Rafe turned as he reached for her hand. He linked their fingers and headed toward Kylie's garage. The door was open, which Odette figured wasn't unusual in this safe neighborhood.

"Stay behind me," Rafe leaned in and whispered before stopping at the door to the house. He pulled her closer to him before putting his ear to the door to listen.

After a few beats of silence, he reached for the handle. The man didn't make a sound as he turned the knob, and then took a step inside.

Odette did her best to follow suit. She suppressed a gasp as they stepped into the kitchen.

Kylie sat in a chair in the middle of the room, hands tied behind her back, with a gun pointed at her right temple. Her eyes widened when she saw them.

"Don't do anything stupid, Spencer," Rafe warned, dropping her hand to put both of his in the air, palms facing out. "I'm not armed."

"Close the door and let me see your cell phones," Spencer demanded. Sweat dripped down the side of his face and his hand shook. His gaze shifted to Odette. "And then let me see your hands too."

Odette reached inside her purse.

"No," Spencer waived the gun, pointing the barrel at her. "Toss your handbag over here on the floor near me."

"Okay," she said, hating the shakiness in her own voice. She slid the strap off her shoulder, crouched down, and then pushed the purse toward him before standing up again. Movement caused pain to shoot up her back. She made a move to place her right hand on her hip but was quickly reminded that was a bad idea.

"Hands up," Spencer demanded. The hysterical quality to his voice had her worried he might accidentally fire the gun.

Odette did as directed. A cramp threatened to double her over, but she was determined not to give him a reason to shoot. He might panic, causing his finger to twitch. Then, boom.

Strangely enough, she wasn't worried about herself in that moment. All she cared about was the baby's health and staying alive to take care of Andie.

Rafe slid his cell phone across the expensive tile flooring toward Spencer.

Hands in the air, Rafe slowly stood up. He glanced over at Odette. A look of concern darkened his features.

"Are you okay?" he asked, turning his full attention to her as she felt the blood drain from her face.

"I will be," she whispered.

"What are you two talking about?" Spencer asked, his high pitch a sign his stress levels were increasing by the second.

Rafe turned to Spencer. "You haven't done anything that you can't recover from yet."

"What's that supposed to mean?" Spencer asked as he reached on top of the counter. The object he was going for was behind a big bowl of fruit, so Odette couldn't make out.

"I'm just saying that you can make this right," he continued.

Spencer tossed duct tape over toward them. It landed with a smack on the tile. "Wrap his arms behind his back."

"What are you doing?" Rafe asked. "Emile wouldn't want this."

"Leave my cousin out of this," Spencer shot back with the venom of the rattler from earlier. "She's gone. My uncle's gone. There will be a family suicide pact and I will be the only one who survives."

"Let Odette go," Rafe said. "She has nothing to do with this."

Spencer glanced down at Kylie. It was just a split-second of eye contact but it sent chills racing down Odette's back.

"If you think I'm allowing that bastard child she's carrying to come after the money, you have another think coming," Spencer stated.

Odette didn't like the sound of any of this. And the brief exchange between Spencer and Kylie left her with questions. Given the circumstances, Odette wondered if she was seeing something that wasn't there.

"Tie her up," Spencer said, his voice rising another couple of octaves. "Do it, now."

She wondered if he would have the same bravado when talking to Rafe if he was the one with the gun.

"I can't do that," Rafe said with a tone that was a study in calm. "It might not be good for the baby."

Spencer practically vibrated with anger. "You can and you will. Or I'll shoot all of you right now, put the gun in your hand, and then stab myself with a knife."

"There's a problem with that plan, Spencer," Rafe continued. "The gunpowder residue will be on your fingers, not mine."

Spencer's gaze immediately dropped to Kylie, as though looking for confirmation or a new direction.

And that's when it dawned on Odette. Kylie was in on this.

"Shoot them both, baby," Kylie said, almost magically breaking free from the bindings. "You don't need me anymore as a decoy."

Spencer's gaze bounced from her to the gun in his hand. He shook his head. "What if he's telling the truth? I told you that I'm not going back to—"

"Listen to Kylie and you'll be back behind bars, Spencer," Rafe continued. "I guarantee it."

"No, baby," she said, standing up and then stepping behind Spencer.

Odette could almost hear Rafe's blood reaching a boiling point.

"You," Rafe said to Kylie. "It's not worth it."

"He had to go," Kylie defended. "This was easier than me leaving. Cleaner. He couldn't come after me."

Kylie had endured some type of abuse from her husband. That much was clear. But to have an affair with her nephew and then kill her husband? Odette wondered how much of the abuse story was real and how much was exaggerated. After everything her own mother had been through, it made Odette sick to her stomach to think someone could lie about something this serious to cover up murder.

"I c-c-c-can't," Spencer said, setting the gun down on top of the countertop. He backed away as Kylie cursed.

And then Rafe dove toward the weapon.

∽

KYLIE REACHED FOR THE GUN. Rafe's shoulder slammed into the counter as he pushed to beat her to it. Their hands collided, knocking the weapon out of reach. It skidded across the granite, flew off the island, and then collided with the tile.

He winced, half expecting it to discharge. A stray bullet could do a whole lot of damage.

Spencer was frozen, but Kylie fought. She dug her nails into the skin of Rafe's cheeks. He grabbed her by the arms and spun her around to face the opposite direction. A cold trickle said she'd drawn blood but he didn't care.

"Spence, baby, get the gun," she said. "Our future. Our plans." She managed to get the words out through gasps.

As Rafe wrapped his arms around her, pinning hers to her sides. She lifted her feet off the ground and tried to kick.

From the corner of his eye, he saw Odette ducking around the island. A few seconds later, she came up with the gun.

"It's over," Rafe stated as Kylie tried to wriggle out of his grip.

"Not so fast," a male voice said from the French doors leading to the backyard.

Rafe turned to get a good look. It was the runner, and he had a gun pointed directly at Odette.

"Let Kylie go, or I'll kill your wife," he said in a cold, detached voice. His hoodie was pulled tight around his face, making it almost impossible to get a clear view of his features.

The guy was young, close to Spencer's age if Rafe had to guess. He also figured the guy had been promised some kind of cut for being involved.

"Der—"

"I told you not to say my name," the runner admonished. "Don't just stand there. Do something."

Spencer shook his head, turned toward the garage and ran. Odette stepped in his path, stopping him. It was a move Rafe wished she hadn't done for her sake. The thought of anything happening to her caused white-hot anger to boil inside him. An ache formed in his chest. This was more than just the thought of losing Emile's baby. This was the thought of losing Odette.

"Emile wouldn't want this, Spencer," Rafe repeated as the younger man stopped five feet in front of the barrel of the gun in Odette's hand.

A truly remorseful look crossed his features.

"I'm sorry," he said as he shook his head.

"You know she wouldn't," Rafe continued, figuring this was the most ground he'd made since arriving. "She cared about you."

Spencer brought his hands up to his head and grabbed fistfuls of his own hair. "I don't know what to do." He squeezed his eyes shut. "She said she loved me but then I thought she loved my uncle too."

"Shut the hell up, Spencer," Kylie demanded as she continued to fight against Rafe's viselike grip.

"I can't," Spencer said, still wearing the same shirt from two days ago. Had the young man even slept? "You poisoned him."

Rafe's mind snapped back to the open cupboard at the townhouse. Did she have the same plan for him and Odette? Did she not care about her grandchild?

He tightened his grip around her to hold her still.

"How could you do this to Emile's baby too?" Spencer asked, remorse written all over his face.

Odette kept the gun trained on him but steadily moved toward her handbag. She slowly bent down and retrieved her cell phone with eyes on Spencer the entire time as Rafe moved in between her and the runner with the gun. She was so close that he could reach out and grab the cell if he wanted to.

But the remorse in Spencer's eyes told Rafe that wasn't going to happen.

"Put the phone down or I swear I'll kill you all," the runner threatened, taking a sidestep to get a better aim.

"It's too late," Rafe said, spinning around to use Kylie's body as a shield. It meant turning his back on Spencer. "Make the call, Odette."

"Spence," the runner said. "What the hell? You got me into this. Now you're just going to hang us all? For what?"

The runner backed up toward the French doors, and then he disappeared.

"Get the tape," Rafe ordered Spencer, unsure if he would do as told.

Surprisingly, Spencer obeyed. He dropped down, held Kylie's feet together and then duct-taped them. He did the same with her arms before securing her to the chair.

Once the threat was neutralized, Rafe took off after the runner figuring the guy would disappear for a long time if he got away.

Possibly never to be found again. The runner was just as guilty, and justice needed to be served.

"I'll be back," he said as he ran after the guy.

## 19

"What have we done?" Spencer dropped to his knees on the tile, and started rocking back and forth.

Odette wanted to comfort him on some level. He was young and thought he was in love. As long as she didn't focus on the fact he was having an affair with his favorite uncle's wife, she could drum up sympathy.

Kylie was clearly conniving, and Spencer had been out of his league. He had a troubled past that Kylie must have used in her favor.

Had she even been abused by her husband? Or was all that a ploy for sympathy too?

It made Odette sick.

"M-m-m-m," Kylie muttered while her mouth was duct taped. Her not being able to speak was probably for the best. She might still have Spencer under some type of spell. The kid was clearly torn up about his actions.

Keeping Kylie quiet was Odette's best chance to get out of this situation alive. For the baby's sake. For Andie's sake.

For Rafe's sake. He deserved to have the baby Odette was carrying. He was going to be an amazing father.

A little piece of her broke at the fact she wouldn't be there to share the child with him. She'd grown to love the little bean. Love?

Yes, she decided. There was no use denying the fact she loved the baby growing inside her as well as the child's father.

But neither option was realistic or on the table so there was no point in focusing on it.

Sirens split the air. Help was on the way.

Spencer looked to panic. He lifted his face. His gaze darted from the back door to the hallway leading to the garage.

"Don't think about it, Spencer," Odette warned. "It'll only make life worse for you. They'll catch you at some point and then they'll throw the book at you. Cooperate and you'll get a lighter sentence."

"I can't believe I went along with killing my uncle," he said, the rocking intensified.

At this point, she feared he might blow before law enforcement arrived. She'd never shot a human being before and doubted she could unless her life was immediately in danger.

She hoped it wouldn't come to that.

"I've been in trouble with the law before," she admitted, trying to establish common ground. "When I was younger."

Spencer locked gazes with her, a frenzied look in his eyes. That wasn't good. She lifted the barrel of the gun to make sure he knew she meant business, praying she wouldn't have to pull the trigger.

Besides, he didn't know how much she wanted to avoid shooting him. She could work with his lack of information.

"What happened?" he asked, looking truly curious.

"I served time in juvie, just like you," she admitted. "But then I turned my life around and here I am."

"Having my cousin's baby," he said with red-rimmed eyes and the most pitiful look on his face.

Could she get him talking about Emile?

"Were the two of you close?" she asked, rubbing her belly with her free hand.

"I looked up to her," Spencer said. "She was nice to me."

"She sounds like an amazing person," Odette continued, liking the fact she seemed to be making ground.

Spencer nodded as Kylie ramped up her protests. Thankfully, she was wearing the equivalent of a muzzle. The tape across her mouth kept her from swaying Spencer in a different direction.

"Tell me about her," she said.

Spencer clamped his mouth shut. For a few long seconds, Odette thought she might have gone too far. Then came, "She would never harm a hair on anyone's body. I can tell you that much for sure. Once, she had me capture a spider in a jar so I could release it out the front door."

Odette smiled as she lowered the gun.

"Emile was like that. You know?" he asked.

She nodded.

"She was just kind," he said. "When other people in the family shunned me after I got into trouble, she talked her dad into taking me in."

"What a nice thing to do," she said with compassion.

"Yeah? And look how I repay him. Her." Spencer looked like he was about to rage out of control.

"That wasn't all your fault," she reassured.

Before he could respond, a knock at the front door

sounded before it swung open and a pair of officers came rushing in.

Odette set her weapon on the tile and backed away. She put her hands in the air. "I'm the one who called."

~

RAFE HAD no plans to let the runner get away this time. The young man fired a wild shot in Rafe's direction but the bullet trajectory went wide.

He couldn't stand the thought of innocent bystanders getting caught up in the crossfire.

"Stop," he commanded. It was wishful thinking on his part as he closed in on the runner.

The young man ramped up his speed. Rafe pushed his thighs harder until he was within arm's reach from the runner.

And then he took a risk and dove, tackling the guy from behind.

The pair landed on the hard earth and rolled. The weapon in the runner's hand flew. Thankfully, it didn't discharge.

"This is it," Rafe said in the younger man's ear as he wrapped his arms and legs around the guy to stop him from scrambling to his feet. "You're not getting away this time."

Rafe wrapped a powerful arm around the guy's neck and squeezed until his body went limp. He retrieved the gun, relieved the middle school wrestling move did the trick with the runner. Rafe was able to stand up, throw the guy over his shoulder caveman style, and walk back toward the house.

As he neared the garage, his heart pounded against his ribcage. A law enforcement SUV was parked out front, lights blaring. He couldn't be certain what he would be walking into.

The minute he set foot in the house, he said, "My name is Rafe Firebrand. One of the guys involved in the murder ran off and I'd like to turn him over to the law. I'm unarmed."

"Hands in the air when you come inside the room," an unfamiliar voice demanded.

"I'd love to, but I'm carrying the perp," he said.

An officer appeared in the mouth of the hallway, gun pointed at Rafe. "Drop him."

Rafe laid the runner down on the tile before slowly putting his hands in the air.

"He's with me," Odette said as she stepped into view. "He's one of the good guys."

Before Rafe could say hello, an officer had the runner in zip cuffs.

"You. Against the wall," the officer said.

Rafe did as told. He was quickly patted down before being deemed clear.

Odette practically ran to him, cradling her bump. In that moment, he realized he wanted to be a family. *With her.*

But he had no idea if she felt the same as she ran into his waiting arms.

After statements were given, arrests were made, and the dust settled, he knew that he needed to tell Odette how he felt about her.

Without saying a word, he drove back to the townhouse. They were safe here now as he helped her out of the truck. She immediately wrapped her arms around him right there in the garage.

"I have something I need to say to you," she said with her face buried in his chest.

"You go first," he urged.

"I wasn't trying to, but somewhere along the line I fell for you, Rafe. Hard. As in, I'm in love with you. And I know that's not part of the job, so I should probably leave before it gets weird," she said. Her words coming out in a rush.

"What if I don't want you to go?" he asked.

"I just think it would be for the best," she continued, not looking up.

So, he cupped her chin in his hand, tilted her face to make eye contact, and said, "I mean, I don't ever want you to go, Odette. I'm in love with you. And I know it's the real deal because I've never felt like this about anyone else before. I don't want you to go because I want you to marry you." He hesitated, wondering if he'd gone too far, too fast. "Whenever you're ready, though. Not now. I know this is a lot to digest. We could maybe date if that's what you need. But I'm certain that I'm head over heels in love with you and I want to spend the rest of our lives together if that's something you want too."

"I've never been any more certain of anything in my life," Odette said, lifting her gaze to lock onto his. "I'm in love with you, Rafe. I want to wake up to you every single morning. And I want to go to bed with you each night."

"We'll be skipping a few steps," he said as his heart threatened to jump from his chest. "Going straight to family mode."

"Sounds perfect to me," she said with a smile that melted every single one of his concerns. As long as she was ready to walk through life together, they could get through anything. "You know I have Andie to care for."

"I'm not afraid," he said. "In fact, she's part of you and the mother you loved. There's no way that I won't love her like a daughter."

"Good," she said, rubbing her belly, "because that will make two."

## 20

EPILOGUE

Consider Morgan Firebrand's mind blown. Never in a million years did he think his brother Rafe would be getting married, let alone having his late fiancée's child. The call from his brother that had come in a couple of weeks ago had been a shock, but Morgan was thrilled for his brother. And now he was on his way to the hospital because Odette was in labor. Another Firebrand was coming into the world, and the family was gathering.

Morgan's cell buzzed, indicating a text. He glanced at the screen as soon as he stopped at a red light. *A girl. Amelia.*

His chest squeezed and a foreign feeling took hold. He'd never been sappy about babies before, so why now?

It was next to impossible to think of his brother as a father. And yet, he'd sounded the happiest he'd ever been on their phone call. Rafe and Odette were in love and planning a wedding. Marriage. A baby. Those were all good things for Rafe.

As for Morgan?

Hell would freeze over before he would consider getting

hitched at this point in his life. He prayed he wouldn't eat those words anytime soon.

Keep reading to find out if Morgan changes his mind about falling in love.

## ALSO BY BARB HAN

**Texas Firebrand**

Rancher to the Rescue

Disarming the Rancher

Rancher under Fire

Rancher on the Line

Undercover with the Rancher

Rancher in Danger

Set-Up with the Rancher

Rancher Under the Gun

Taking Cover with the Rancher

**Firebrand Cowboys**

VAUGHN: Firebrand Cowboys

RAFE: Firebrand Cowboys

MORGAN: Firebrand Cowboys

NICK: Firebrand Cowboys

**Don't Mess With Texas Cowboys**

Texas Cowboy's Protection

Texas Cowboy Justice

Texas Cowboy's Honor

Texas Cowboy Daddy

Texas Cowboy's Baby

Texas Cowboy's Bride

Texas Cowboy's Family

Texas Cowboy Sheriff

Texas Cowboy Marshal

Texas Cowboy Lawman

Texas Cowboy Officer

Texas Cowboy K9 Patrol

**Cowboys of Cattle Cove**

Cowboy Reckoning

Cowboy Cover-up

Cowboy Retribution

Cowboy Judgment

Cowboy Conspiracy

Cowboy Rescue

Cowboy Target

Cowboy Redemption

Cowboy Intrigue

Cowboy Ransom

For more of Barb's books, visit www.BarbHan.com.

## ABOUT THE AUTHOR

Barb Han is a USA TODAY and Publisher's Weekly Bestselling Author. Reviewers have called her books "heartfelt" and "exciting."

Barb lives in Texas—her true north—with her adventurous family, a poodle mix, and a spunky rescue who is often referred to as a hot mess. She is the proud owner of too many books (if there is such a thing). When not writing, she can be found exploring new cities, on a mountain either hiking or skiing depending on the season, or swimming in her own backyard.

Sign up for Barb's newsletter at www.BarbHan.com.

Printed in Great Britain
by Amazon